D1376266

Bordeaux, Private Eye
by
Rorie Smith

Tan Tan Books 2021

Edited by Sarah Dawes
Cover image by romi49/Shutterstock
Tan Tan Books, Freathy, Cornwall.
Website: tantanbooks.co.uk
Email: editor@tantanbooks.co.uk

TAN TAN BOOKS 2021
REPRINTED 2021
ISBN: 978-0-992950-34-7

For Jeanne, as ever …

… And with thanks also to all in the NHS who battled so heroically
to save us during the pandemic.

Bordeaux, Private Eye
What the Critics Said:

DELIGHTUL: 'This novel is delightful, really imaginative and clever.'

Dee Burton, author of I Dream of Woody

COMIC GENIUS: 'When I was sent Bordeaux, Private Eye for appraisal I read the whole thing over one weekend and loved it. Rorie Smith takes a literary line for a walk round a clutch of believable and endearing, if eccentric, characters with surreal sub-plots deftly woven through. This is genre-defying comic genius with a twist in the tail, not so much a 'whodunnit' as a 'who did they do it to'. The most fun I've had at work for a long time.'

Sarah Dawes, Editor

CURIOUS: 'A curious blend of humour, drama, and suspense.'

Oliver Tooley, Blue Poppy Publishing, Devon, UK

PHILOSOPHICAL: 'Bordeaux, Private Eye is an engaging, sometimes improbable novel, which is nonetheless a genuine page-turner. Improbable because it weaves the Queen of England and her social circle into the narrative, yet it still stands as a compelling tale of a philosophical waterfront street photographer and his beautiful circus acrobat wife. It explores the nature of society's power structure and why rebellions against its partiality and unfairness fall so far short of being anyway remedial. Which asks the despairing question: Is what we've got as good as it gets?'

Christy McCormick, Editor, Hong Kong Shipping Gazette, former literary editor of the Montreal Gazette

SURREAL: 'There is an odd appeal about this surreal little book that defies pigeon-holing. As the title suggests (or perhaps it doesn't), it's sort of a detective story set in Bordeaux, mostly. At times it's hard to tell. With all its twists, sub-stories and asides, the narrative seems to be acting a part itself and daring the reader to stay on the trail of the plot. Perseverance pays off as the main characters, photographers-turned-sleuths Bill and Polly Smith, get their teeth into their subject amid all the diversions. The writing flows and keeps the intertwined stories moving along at pace. It's short enough to finish in one sitting, which could be a good idea – to avoid getting lost in a book the wrong way!'

Chuck Grieve, Editor, Mosaique Press, Dordogne, France

QUIRKY: 'Don't expect a conventional amateur sleuth story here! This is a distinctly different and quirky stroll through Bordeaux as Bill Smith and his wife track what they think could be wrongdoing. There are diversions along the way: to the Arctic, followed by a sideways look at some senior members of the Establishment in England and speculation on what really did happen to Goya's head. The author lives in Bordeaux and his knowledge and enjoyment of the city (and its cakes) is evident. Great fun for those who know it and will probably make those who have never been feel like visiting.'

Victoria Corby, Times bestselling author

ATTRACTIVELY ECCENTRIC: 'There are recurrent themes in Rorie Smith's books: an active but despairing anti-Populist/Establishment stance; a cast of the attractively eccentric but generally unambitious; an obsession with location; that all of the above should make you laugh. While I've loved all of his previous books I have wondered whether those themes might be too strong to keep some reading. So, if you're tempted to take the plunge this is the book as you can take it as a light read in whatever your favourite genre is; thriller, romance, character, place, twist or comedy – take your pick. Yet the underlying obsessions are still there and I think you'll want to pick up another of Rorie's books and regret not doing so sooner. But if you do take the plunge, don't forget the tidal currents ...'

'Merluza', former Waterstones manager, Devon, UK

The writer Martin Amis quotes his father, the novelist Kingsley Amis, as saying in his later years, 'I'm not going to read any more novels that don't begin with the sentence, "A shot rang out."'

CHAPTER ONE

A shot rang out … and a body fell into the water.

Bill Smith looked up from the typewriter. He shook his head, looked down and tried again.

A shot rang out … and Bill Smith fell into the water.

Bill Smith sat back. He frowned. Better, but still not right. He tried a third time.

A shot rang out … and Bill Smith, giving a howl of pain and anger and clutching his arm to staunch the flow of blood from the bullet wound, fell into the water.

Bill Smith sat back. He tapped his pencil against the old Underwood typewriter. Better to start a few frames back.

Bill Smith was walking along the Quais when he noted a man with a gun on top of the warehouse. The gun glinted in the early morning sunlight.

That built up the suspense.

But whichever way you start, unless you back up Bill Smith to where he is getting out of bed that morning, scratching his … etc., etc., you always hit on that blocker of an opening sentence. Bill Smith leaned back in his chair and sucked the end of a pencil for a long moment. Perhaps it would be better to

1

go off in another direction altogether. After a moment's pause, and with a smile touching the corners of his lips, he leaned forward and started typing again.

The last time Roger the Diplomat had tea with the Queen she leaned over, tapped him on the knee and asked, 'What's it all about then, Roger?'

Now, that had possibilities. He continued, gaining confidence as he typed.

Roger had only just returned from his most recent assignment in Japan and so had barely enough time to go through the papers to get up to speed on the resignation before he got the call that Elizabeth wanted to see him. Naturally, he drove straight up to Sandringham, where she gave him tea in a private sitting room overlooking the park.

'Well, Elizabeth …' He hesitated, trying to think where to start. He and Elizabeth went back a long way and she often relied on him for 'man of the world' explanations but this was a difficult one.

The long and short of it was that the PM had been caught in a compromising position in a Brussels nightclub. The details were rather salacious. In what the newspapers called a 'moment of madness' the PM had got up onto the stage in the Devil's Dungeon. Then, according to the reports, she had stripped down to her underwear and danced the cancan with the Prime Minister of the Czech Republic. Of course, when the footage emerged on the internet she had to go. There could be no doubt about that. The usual excuses for bad behaviour were made: a momentary lapse, stress, a low tolerance to alcohol. Some commentators even suggested her drink may have been spiked.

Roger's attempts at an explanation – that it was a difficult time and that the negotiations were going badly – didn't convince Elizabeth. She reminded him that she had her own problems with Charles (whom, *entre nous*, she still refers to as 'young Jug Ears') but that she still behaved responsibly. Roger waited a few moments before trying to lighten the rather sombre mood by telling her a funny story he had picked up in Tokyo about the Japanese prime minister. Apparently he had got the tail of his coat caught in a lift door as he was on his way to an official function, with the consequences you can imagine. That had made her laugh.

After that, as she often did in those days – it was well into autumn, evening had fallen and the sitting room was cosy with a warming fire – Elizabeth started to reminisce. In the end they returned, as Roger knew they would, to the story of Harold Macmillan, his wife Dorothy and the awful Bob Boothby. It is a story which, astonishingly, even brings in a serial killer by the unlikely name of John Bodkin Adams! It is a story which still could, if certain details were revealed, lead to what the journalists call a 'Grave Constitutional Crisis'. So it behoves us all to be careful.

Bill Smith stopped typing. He had heard a key turning in the lock and knew that his beloved Polly Smith had returned home.

'Cootcha coo,' he called out. 'Cootcha coo,' she called back.

It was only later that evening, an hour before going to bed, that Bill Smith was once again able to resume his position at the old Underwood typewriter – to find to his annoyance that he had completely lost his train of thought. So, casting around for a way back into the story, he typed: Bill Smith met his wife in a Starbucks cafe.

At the time, he wrote, he had been a production manager at a commercial photo laboratory and had been in the habit of taking his break in a nearby Starbucks.

Bill Smith has been criticised for patronising a company like Starbucks, especially in such a grand city as ours, which has dozens of excellent locally owned cafes. In his defence Bill

Smith always quotes our home-grown philosopher Michel de Montaigne: 'We are all patchwork and so shapeless and diverse in composition that each bit, each moment, plays its own game.'

We all know how Starbucks works, Bill Smith typed. You order your coffee and they ask your name. Your name is then written on the empty paper cup that will eventually hold your coffee. When your coffee is ready your name is called out and you step forward to the pickup area to collect.

Now, to set the scene for what followed, we should say that Bill Smith was born William Smith. But over the years he has grown into a Bill Smith; he has the slightly crumpled shirt and the emerging pot belly and the hair that always looks like it needs a comb through. And, like thousands of other Bill Smiths and Harry Browns and Walter Greens, he just about gets by. He even has the Bill Smith shuffle. They all have it, just like they all got the school report that read, 'Bill should assert himself more.'

It's well known that William Smiths are a sparkier and classier bunch.

But, Bill Smith typed, on that day he had no inkling of anything unusual to come. It was a day like any other. He was on a quick fifteen-minute break from the photo lab; it was just time enough for a coffee and a sit down and a bit of a ponder. He thought, when he looked back, that the changing season could have been an unconscious influence. After a long winter, there was the first hint of renewal in the air. New shoots starting to pop up. Spring around the corner. All that sort of stuff.

So anyhow, Bill Smith typed, Bill Smith placed his order and the server held up the paper cup and said, 'Name, sir?' Bill Smith opened his mouth, as you do, to say 'Bill Smith' but instead – to his surprise and in a voice that was un-Bill-Smith-

4

like in its boldness and clarity – he heard himself sing out, 'My name is Sir Winston Churchill.'

Well, the girl looked at Bill Smith and said, 'Huh?'

People who work in Starbucks don't get much history. He could have backed down then and said something like 'Win' or 'Church' and that would have been the end of his little rebellion, snuffed out even before it started. But instead he doubled down. He leaned over the counter and spelled out the name slowly and watched as she wrote down all three words.

The guy at the pickup counter was smarter and got the joke. When the hot beverage (as they call it in America) was ready, he called out in a loud voice, 'Sir Winston Churchill.' As you can imagine, heads turned. And Bill Smith swore his shoulders went back and his chest jutted forward as he walked up to the counter.

After that Bill Smith got into the swing of it. He started to dress for the part. One day he was Napoleon Bonaparte and the next day he was George Gershwin. When he declared himself Lawrence of Arabia at a Starbucks in a part of town with a large immigrant population people turned to look. He lost weight and bought half a dozen new shirts and a new jacket. He got a decent haircut and shaved off the moustache.

And he even started to have a bit of success with the ladies, Bill Smith typed. Figure it: you shuffle in as plain old Bill Smith, head down and shirt all creased and, well, who's going to take note. But sport a nice titfer and step smartly forward with your well-shined shoes when the server calls out, 'Frappuccino for General Charles de Gaulle,' and people are going to notice. Of course it wasn't long before others started to copy him. In fact, for a short time, it became quite the mode.

But on the day it happened, things were not going particularly well. He was starting to run out of famous names. When the server called out, 'Skinny latte for Chancellor

Konrad Adenauer,' it was hardly surprising that no one batted an eyelid.

So, Bill Smith was sitting there minding his business and thinking about nothing much, except probably that he should get back to the photo lab, when his eye was caught by the back of a girl in a stunning white evening dress. The ensemble was topped by a large white hat. And when the server called out, 'Flat white for Miss Marilyn Monroe,' and she turned round ... Well, as soon as their eyes connected Bill Smith was smitten.

Her name was Polly Brown and she had worked, among other things, as a photographer's model. She had also been 'something or other' in the circus. But that was the start of their life together.

CHAPTER TWO

Bill Smith rolls back the paper in the old Underwood typewriter. In the excitement of starting a new story he has omitted to give either a location or a season.

The city is Bordeaux, one of the great cities of France. (A city recently restored to its former glory by Mayor Alain Juppé, affectionately known among the citizens as the Sun King.) The season is autumn, towards the end of September. The days are still warm and the colourful cruise boats are still coming up the Garonne to moor at the Quais in the heart of the city but the dreadful heat of August is behind us. This is all happening before the Great Plague strikes: that time when we could dance and mingle and mix and jet off for a weekend at a whim, not realising that old Nature was sitting there biding her time and getting ready to teach us a lesson.

So now, as they say, we are 'oriented' so we can continue.

Bill Smith is browsing through the quirky theatrical outfitters that nestles discreetly behind the church in Mérignac. In the window the proprietor has put up a handwritten sign which reads, 'Providers of Costumes for Amateur Theatricals, Fancy Dress Parties and Whatever Else Takes Your Fancy.'

After a root through, Bill Smith has found a bicorn hat that will serve as a replacement for the one that got bashed the other day. (An incident that he will recount later, time and space allowing.)

Pleased with his purchase, Bill Smith has boarded the tram going back into the city. The tram is rattling past Fontaine d'Arlac and approaching the Boulevard. As they near the city, the tram fills up; soon it will be standing room only. When the doors open at Peychotte a blast of hot late-afternoon air enters the tram. Outside, the light is still bright and intense. Pedestrians still hug patches of shade.

This account will not, in the normal way, go on about the great heat that is coming, i.e. climate change. Though, Bill Smith types, if there is space he will have a pop at Mayor Alain Juppé for allowing those seventeen healthy chestnut trees to be cut down on Place Gambetta. Polly Smith said she was going to chain herself to a tree as a protest but in the end they came and cut them down early in the morning when all the protesters, including Bill and Polly Smith, were still asleep in their beds. When Polly Smith walked past later in the day and saw the felled trees lying there, like so many dead bodies, she said it was as if she had stumbled on the site of a massacre. Overall, can we say just a general 'mea culpa' to future generations? By our stupidity we have ruined the planet and you are correct to regard us with contempt.

Also, as previously stated, this account was written before the advent of the Great Plague. But everything written about the dangers of climate change could apply equally well to the Great Plague.

Bill Smith stops typing and looks up. He reads back over the last paragraphs. Should he scrap everything written so far and turn it into a story on climate change, this being of primordial importance? In the end he decides against, arguing to himself that in the coming catastrophe a little light relief might be needed.

Bill Smith sits thinking for a long moment. Then he writes: to be judged a success, a modern novel has to be as rigid as sheet metal in its construction, while at the same time as complex as the Hampton Court maze in its delivery.

He gives the following example of a story proposal that would certainly be rejected by a publisher.

A man is brought before a court on a charge. He gives his name as Ludovic April and his profession as literary critic. He is in his mid-twenties, dishevelled, unshaven, hair not combed. He is walking with the aid of a cane which, the court usher notices, has a silver top engraved in the shape of a griffin. When asked by the judge to explain his extraordinary actions, Ludovic April leans forward and replies in a mellifluous Welsh baritone, 'It was me unconscious what made me do it, guv.'

This will be turned down for being rambling, discursive, offbeat and frankly 'old hat'. The same fate will probably await this literary endeavour, Bill Smith adds. But in Bill Smith's opinion a story can go where it likes and do what it wants as long as it holds the reader's attention. If it fails to do that, then it should certainly be closed up, put to one side and something more interesting picked up. (In this instance, Dear Reader, there is a 'bump' coming soon, when a criminal element will be introduced. So please do try to stay with us.)

Bill Smith gets up and goes into the kitchen to get a drink of water. When he returns he sits down to write some more.

Sometimes, when the tram is not busy, Bill Smith stands up at the front and watches the driver. Whenever he reads of an accident on the tramway in *Sud Ouest* it always ends with the same last line, '... and the driver was taken to hospital suffering from shock.' Oh yes, you can see that. It takes time for these monsters to stop and there are no barriers. So the driver sees the stranded car fifty metres ahead. But all he can do is slam on the brakes and then watch in horror as the accident, which frequently turns into a death drama, unfolds in slow motion.

Bill Smith looks out of the window to his left and sees that they are passing the wall of the Chartreuse Cemetery. This reminds him of the story of Goya's head.

Actually that could interest a publisher, Bill Smith types. It's got art and mystery and is so long ago it can't possibly offend. It could also be turned into a film, which is a financial advantage.

A proposal, Bill Smith writes, could start with a suitably dramatic line such as, 'The French and Spanish officials, partially shrouded by a low-hanging early morning mist, are stamping their feet to keep warm as the gravediggers hack down into the frozen ground.'

Background notes would have to be given, so Bill Smith adds: Francisco Goya (Spanish painter), buried in the Chartreuse Cemetery (1828). Had moved north to Bordeaux four years previously, after falling foul of the Spanish authorities in Madrid. But political wheels turn and Goya's reputation is rehabilitated. So, sixty years on (1888), Madrid wants its great painter hero back. Hence the exhumation.

The pitch continues: the gravediggers, with much huffing and puffing, finally bring up the coffin and remove the lid. The officials peer forward – and then take smart steps back. Our Spanish national hero and genius painter is minus his head!

That is the pitch, the catch, the hook that will get the publishers and the film producers on board. The Hunt for Goya's Head! The advantage of fiction over fact is that the head can be discovered wherever publishers and film producers think it most beneficial to them.

But in this case there are other interesting facts on which the fiction can be mounted. For instance, the gravediggers really do discover a note in the coffin. It is tucked away in a leather pouch in the space where the head should be. The note explains that the head has been removed by a certain Dr G, who has passed it to a certain Professor B at the École de Médecine de Bordeaux. The plan is to study the head to find the source of Goya's genius.

Bill Smith shifts his position on the seat as the tram leaves the Chartreuse Cemetery behind.

In the next scene the head (now a skull), having been fully studied, is about to be discarded. But at the last moment it's rescued by a student who takes it to the Sol y Sombra, a Spanish cafe in Bordeaux situated next to the Capucins market. The cafe owner places the skull on a raised dais in a back parlour. Word passes round and soon expatriate Spaniards from all over the city are turning up to pay homage to the great man.

For the final scene we fast forward to the mid-1950s. The popular press of the day is reporting what they call a 'crime of passion' at the Sol y Sombra. Doors close, business shuts up. Fixtures and fittings, including skull of Goya, all sold off at the flea market in Mériadeck. And this (for the time being at least) is the last anyone hears of Goya's skull …

The tram is rattling past the end of the cemetery wall now.

Bill Smith takes a coin from his pocket. Flips it over. It comes up heads. So now Bill Smith knows where the story is going next.

There is never an ideal time to introduce Carl Jung and his theory of synchronicity into a story. This is because many people regard it as just a clever way to talk about coincidence. Or, if you like, the incidence of coincidence. To put it visually, if the world were a lake and the lake were drained what you would see on the dried-out lake floor would not just be a random selection of old trees and earthy hummocks and dead grass and mud and a few floundering fish and so on. What you would be able to observe would be specific lines, patterns and connections. So a lot of things that are inexplicable today would become explicable. In other words everything is connected up.

Goya's missing head is a good example.

In his later years Goya's speciality was etchings of terrible war scenes. He engraved hundreds of images of mutilated soldiers and civilians with arms and legs smashed up. There are also quite a few with heads off-chopped. And now there he is himself, the great Spanish painter lying in his coffin – and this time it's his own head that has been off-chopped. As Dr Jung might say, 'It's not rocket science, old boy. Just join up the dots.'

Bill Smith, looking out of the window of the tram, has a sudden image of a man in a garage. The man is preparing a car bomb or a barrel bomb. Then he stops and looks at a picture pinned to the wall. It is a magazine reproduction of the Goya picture that everyone knows, the one with the Christ figure being shot by a firing squad. He examines it for a moment and then puts down his bomb-making equipment and walks out of the garage and away.

As a postscript, Polly Smith went to the site of Goya's tomb in the Chartreuse Cemetery last All Saints Day to see if anyone had remembered him. There is still a memorial column there. And, yes someone had left a carefully arranged bowl of colourful flowers with a note reading, in Spanish, 'Our Dear Francisco. Returned Home. Almost.' Polly Smith reckons it was probably a distant relation.

So now the tram on which Bill Smith is riding has passed Mériadeck and is slowing down for Palais de Justice. People are pushed together like the proverbial tinned fishes and Bill Smith is grateful to have his seat. When the tram halts, there is the usual blast of hot air and noises exterior as the doors open. Passengers off-shuffle and new passengers on-bustle.

Bill Smith stops typing. He taps the side of the typewriter with his pencil. He frowns.

Bill Smith could have noted any number of fetching young women, any number of oddly shaped pensioners or strangely clothed immigrants or any one of those gap-toothed children who stare at you open-mouthed. Or he could have simply sat with his eyes closed, ignoring everything. But instead his attention is drawn to two young men carrying attaché cases.

Bill Smith makes his deduction from a partial view. He is sitting down and the young men are standing up so all he can see is their well-shined shoes, their neatly pressed trousers and their thick attaché cases. But the clue is that they have boarded at Palais de Justice. This is the nearest stop to the law courts. So it is odds-on that those thick attaché cases are filled with legal documents. And legal documents are known, of course, to be the deadliest of weapons.

Then Bill Smith has what he calls later a 'stroke of good fortune.' But Polly Smith says she would prefer to substitute 'stroke of good fortune' with 'life-changing moment.' The incident happens at the next stop, which is Hôtel de Ville. There is an exodus of passengers and the young lawyers take the two empty seats directly behind where Bill Smith is sitting.

So Bill Smith leans back. He also closes his eyes which, he says later to Polly Smith, helps him to focus his attention and listen more clearly. And the question is, does he do this deliberately, because he knows instinctively that something important is about to be disclosed? In other words, is it his unconscious calling? Or is it just chance? People on the tram treat a public space as a private space. If you are so inclined you can tune in to any number of private conversations. Only yesterday, Bill Smith had overheard a conversation between a betrayed wife and her lawyer in which surprisingly intimate details of her divorce were discussed.

Polly Smith asks Bill Smith to summarise his first impression of the young lawyers from their voices. Bill Smith considers for a moment and then replies, 'Typical young lawyers. Plum in the mouth and a bit cocksure.'

Bill Smith then recounts to Polly Smith the opening lines of the murder plot. There are no names of course, but Bill Smith says it sounds as though, from the brief conversation he overheard, the intended victim is a young woman. She is either to be pushed off a bridge into the Garonne or held with her head under the water until she drowns.

A shocked Polly Smith says they should go to the police but Bill Smith disagrees, arguing that they need more evidence. Polly Smith then asks about a motive but Bill Smith says he has no idea.

But then he thinks back over the conversation once more.

By the way, Dear Reader, do you know those Jackson Pollock paintings? The ones where everything crosses over and is intertwined? There are people who say the paintings are a good representation of how the brain works.

So now Bill Smith's brain is lighting up like one of those Jackson Pollock paintings. His thoughts are criss-crossing over each other in that chaotic Jackson Pollock manner.

However – and this is interesting – if you do some research you will find that the chaos of a Jackson Pollock painting, those criss-crossing lines or chaotic paint daubs, are not random at all. What Jackson Pollock is doing, the experts say, is unconsciously representing patterns made by old Nature herself. These are patterns that repeat themselves continually up and down the scale, from twig to tree trunk. If you want to get technical they are called fractals. Pollock also underwent sessions of Jungian psychoanalysis, which were a great influence on him. He was also drunk a lot of the time.

But anyhow, that is all a rough way of describing how Bill Smith's brain is working, firing off in all directions. Your brain probably works in the same way. So what is happening is that a tortured thought is making its way down those wiry criss-crossing brain tendrils and when, sputtering like a burning fuse, it makes its way into clear air, Bill Smith realises what has been missing from his analysis is that the two young lawyers are not working alone but are under orders from a third party.

Bill Smith also tells Polly Smith that he is sure he is clocked by one of the lawyers. He has leaned his head back a fraction too far and has been a little too still. People know when someone is listening in to their conversation.

So the lawyers, realising they have been overheard, have abruptly stopped talking. Bill Smith decides to stay on the tram as it passes his normal Sainte-Catherine stop. As casually as he can, he is watching the doors.

As the tram draws into the Place de Bourgogne the two lawyers get up. Bill Smith follows a couple of paces behind, discreet and unassuming as always. That old Bill Smith shuffle can come in useful at times. But as they wait on the crowded platform for the C Line tram that will take them down to the Gare Saint Jean, Bill Smith gets a side-on look at the pair of young lawyers. And his estimation is exactly correct, he tells Polly Smith.

'They are well dressed but in that casual, open-collar manner. It's also the way they stand, looking around with that real confident look.'

Bill Smith names the taller one the Boy. He is the more naive of the two. His face is round and open. His sidekick is smaller and longer in the face. Bill Smith calls him the Fox. He puts them both in their early twenties. Bill Smith notes a dog-eared paperback peeping from the jacket pocket of the Boy and is intrigued to know what it is. The Fox has taken off his jacket but Bill Smith can see in the pocket a rolled up copy of *Sud Ouest*, in which all local events, certainly including any accounts of bodies found floating in rivers, are recorded.

Polly Smith is leaning forward anxiously.

'Do you think they were on to you?'

'We were pretty much cheek by jowl down to the Gare Saint Jean,' Bill Smith replies in the seasoned manner of a private detective long used to following suspects. 'It was standing room only. Afternoon rush. The Fox had certainly clocked my presence. His nose was up. He scented danger. He knew they had been indiscreet.'

When they get off the tram Bill Smith expects them to go into the station for a train out to the country and so he is surprised and rather wrong-footed, he tells Polly Smith, when they cross the road and enter the Café du Levant.

CHAPTER THREE

Bill Smith is so shaken by his encounter with the young lawyers that it is only the following day that he remembers to take the bicorn hat out of its white plastic bag and try it on in front of Polly Smith.

Polly Smith takes a pace back and puts her head to one side.

Bill Smith has not mentioned that Polly Smith has one eye a different colour from the other. The medical term for it is heterochromia iridum. The left eye is a soft blue and the right is hazel brown. Bill Smith finds this devilishly attractive. He says that, taken with her previous career as a circus performer, it makes Polly Smith irresistible.

Polly Smith dresses brightly, with a tendency towards the beatnik and bohemian. She loves a long, trailing scarf and a flowered, theatrical hat. She can be scatty and flirtatious at times, with a rather devil-may-care manner. On occasion, comparisons have been made to Liza Minnelli in her pomp.

So they are quite the odd couple: the extrovert Polly Smith with her circus connections and old hangdog Bill Smith.

Polly Smith adjusts Bill Smith's new bicorn hat. The colour is a rich blue and there is gold tasselling and half a dozen silver stars. After a minute, but in a voice that shows she is not entirely convinced, she says, 'Well, I suppose it will do.'

Bill Smith stops typing and reads back what he has written. He needs to pull the threads together. The account of the Grave Constitutional Crisis will have to be developed. And of course no writer can let a murder plot fizzle out. At the same time, some background is required to 'flesh out' Bill and Polly Smith.

Polly Brown becomes Polly Smith at a simple ceremony at City Hall in Bordeaux. The wedding breakfast afterwards is a real old gathering of Polly Smith's circus 'family'. Bill Smith is introduced to lion tamers, elephant handlers, bareback riders, hunchbacks, dwarves and to one man who is obviously the giant. But, strangely enough, when Polly Smith challenges him to identify the clown he is unable to do so as any one of them could have fitted the bill.

By the way, talking of circuses, did you see the etchings of the German painter Otto Dix at the Tate Modern in London? Like Goya, he draws the horror of war and all the misery it brings. There are plenty of off-chopped heads as well as bodies with other critical parts missing. But he also draws the strangest circus scenes. He has switchbacks and breaks that are all wrong. There are curves where there should be edges, that sort of thing. The etchings certainly ask questions about the laws of gravity and cause and effect and so on. A good title for the etchings would be *Balanced on the Head of a Pin*.

And by the way again, the word 'family' seems to have a loose interpretation among the circus fraternity. There is a lot of the 'cousin' and 'uncle' thing going on. But there is no doubt, whatever Polly Smith's true status, that she is regarded as family.

After the wedding, Bill and Polly Smith take a short honeymoon bicycling in the Béarn and the Gers, which is where they gain a taste for Madiran, a wine of the region. Space allowing, Bill Smith will say more about this later on. Experts are divided on Madiran: some call it 'rude but drinkable' while others dismiss it altogether.

It is on their return from honeymoon that Bill Smith says he cannot stay a moment longer at the commercial photo laboratory and Polly Smith says that the circus is no place for a married woman.

It is actually Polly Smith's idea that they become quayside photographers. She has noted that the number of cruise liners coming up the River Garonne and mooring at the Quais over the summer is increasing. So she says they should offer a service photographing the tourists as they descend the gangplank from their giant tourist boats.

The first thing they do is to buy an African grey parrot. With family in the circus you can get all sorts of things. They are told that the parrot, which is called Popov, can imitate voices, but neither Bill nor Polly Smith ever hears a word from it.

Bill Smith dresses as Long John Silver with the intention that the parrot will perch on his shoulder, but more often than not it ends up perching on Polly Smith's hat. So when one day it slips its securing chain and flies up into the trees on the Place des Quinconces, Polly and Bill Smith say good riddance and buy a stuffed one.

The Smiths would have liked to work with an old-style plate camera with a hood and so on. That would certainly have impressed the tourists, but it is not practical as the developing takes forever and the emphasis today is on speed. They also experiment with a large-format Polaroid camera but eventually choose a newer compact model. The picture is placed in a sleeve on which is printed the inscription 'A Souvenir of Bordeaux' in a dozen different languages.

Over the first summer their costumes go through a variety of iterations. To begin with, Bill Smith dresses as Winston Churchill with bowler hat and cigar and Polly Smith reverts to the Marilyn Monroe costume with which she had first attracted Bill Smith. But it is only when Bill Smith puts on military uniform and bicorn hat in the style of Napoleon Bonaparte and Polly Smith dresses in full skirt as Josephine that they start to have any real success.

But this popularity attracts some rather unwelcome attention from *Sud Ouest*. The paper accuses Bill and Polly Smith of vulgarising the city in front of visitors who have come from all over the world. To which Bill Smith replies that it would be impossible to get anything more vulgar than a large cruise boat, taller than most of the buildings in Bordeaux, disgorging hundreds of tourists, ambling and sheeplike, into the city. Bill Smith also points out in his letter (which Polly Smith says is overly long, showing his tendency to ramble) that Badie, that well-known (and appropriately named) wine emporium on the Allées de Tourny, is offering wine for sale to said sheeplike tourists for in excess of 2,500 euros per bottle! And that is not to mention, Bill Smith continues in the same rather rambling style, the funfair at Place des Quinconces, which sets up at regular intervals directly behind where the cruise boats moor, with its big wheel and its merry-go-round and its carnival barkers. Bill Smith concludes by saying that he and Polly Smith fit in very well alongside all of that! After that, Bill Smith types, there is no more criticism of them in *Sud Ouest* and they become a fixture on the Quais and the fairground.

(As to the first bicorn hat, it is following his dispute with *Sud Ouest* that a group of lively lads, doing it for a dare to impress the girls, tip the hat off Bill Smith's head and kick it around like a football so that, when it is apologetically returned by one of the girls, it is bashed pretty much out of shape.)

Bill Smith stops typing. He looks out of the window.

He had woken in the middle of the night thinking he had got it wrong about those lawyers. Perhaps they had been rehearsing a plot for a novel or a film? Then he recalled those thick attaché cases full of legal documents. Lawyers deal in fact, not fiction. He also hadn't liked the way they had stood on the platform with that real superior look.

Then Bill Smith realises he has offered no explanation as to how Bill Smith, a pot-bellied Englishman, ended up living in Bordeaux. Realising he needs to move the story on, he begins to type rapidly.

Everyone knows the world is all muddled up today with people living hugger-mugger and cheek by jowl. Sometimes they get on and it is hunky dory and lovey lovey and sometimes they don't and there are fights on the streets and all that sort of thing. One thinks of those poor black people who came from the West Indies to London to work after the war, only to find many of the locals did not like them and spat at them in the streets and said they were worse than dogs and that they should all go home. And yet when the Germans arrive, after all they have done, bombing Plymouth and London and all that, no one minds and everyone says, 'Oh the good old Germans, do come in and have a cup of tea.'

Polly Smith says she read in *Sud Ouest* that there are 300,000 French people living in England. Does anyone know what they are all doing there? Are they hanging round street corners making a nuisance of themselves or are they going for what is called today an 'opportunity'?

Which is by way of a preamble to say that Bill Smith's father went from Cornwall, where he had worked in a tin mine at St Just, to Canada for an opportunity. He spent ten years in the mining camps of Northern Quebec, where he liked to say life was cheap and it was all tough as hell and come payday there were fights and the rum flowed and there were loose women, etc., etc. In fact, he worked as a camp cook so he stayed in the warm cookhouse, only poking his nose out of the door every so often for a breath of fresh air and a cigarette. When he was not working he used to lie in his bunk and read the works of the great adventurer Jack London.

But anyhow, when it was time to come home he had become used to French ways in Quebec, so he came to France and settled in Bordeaux. Bill Smith's father liked to tell stories of the Canadian North. These had a great effect on Bill Smith, though he has never visited the Canadian North himself.

Actually, Bill Smith has not been to a lot of places, on the whole being comfortable in his home town. His one attempt at an 'adventure' turned into a misadventure which, space allowing, we will record later.

By the way, Bill and Polly Smith are also great readers and are regular visitors to the library at Mériadeck. In other words they get their thrills by reading in the books there about all the great adventurers. And anyway, the income of a quayside photographer does not allow for Arctic – or desert – expeditions.

And by the way (again) did you know that a wildlife photographer in Africa has recently photographed a black leopard? This is an exceptionally rare thing to do. Bill Smith read about it on the back page of *Sud Ouest*. Bill Smith tells Polly Smith he would have liked to have done something like that. Then people would look back in later years and say, 'Remember old Bill Smith? Made his name in Africa. First chap to photograph a black leopard. Unusual sort of a fellow. Don't make them like that anymore.'

Bill Smith stops and takes a deep breath. That is some background put down at least.

So Bill and Polly Smith are at breakfast the next morning when Bill Smith comes across an interesting snippet on the back page of *Sud Ouest* and says to Polly Smith, 'Listen to this,' and reads out, 'A light plane on a medical evacuation flight has gone missing in Northern Quebec.'

So that evening when they have finished photographing the tourists down on the Quais they tune in, via the internet, to a radio station in Northern Quebec.

Everyone who has read those Jack London books and seen those black-and-white films knows that a search for a downed flyer in the Canadian North always contains a scene where the injured pilot, headphones clamped over ears, taps out a last desperate message on a primitive wireless set. You can also add in howling wolves, frostbitten fingers, crackle and static from the radio and never-ending night to make up the picture. Then, in the last reel, a lonely ham radio operator on a cattle ranch in the Australian outback picks up the final desperate message and alerts the authorities and the rescue is made just in time.

Which is not to make light of a desperate situation, Bill Smith types. He adds, 'If the plane has gone down …' and then stops. If? Well it has certainly gone down by now. Either that or it has been whooshed up into the sky by Martian invaders!

Then Bill Smith opens a drawer and finds, carefully preserved like Goya's head, the maps his father had brought back from Canada. His father had marked on the maps the camps where he had worked. Bill Smith had pored over the maps as a child. They are large scale, with wonderfully evocative names such as Lake of the Lion and Wolf Back Ridge and so on. They are names to make your pulse race. Northern Quebec, Bill Smith types, is a land half-finished, raw and rough, gouged out by the retreating ice.

And here we are once again, back to dear old Carl Jung and his theory of synchronicity. Because what Bill and Polly Smith discover is that the camps where Bill Smith's father worked are right in the middle of the search area! So that is another coincidence to figure out. The maps also show, by the way, that the search area is half the size of France. So they are into quite a game of needles and haystacks.

When Bill and Polly Smith tune into the radio station via the internet they follow the briefings given by what are called the 'authorities'. They are very soon on top of the situation even though they are 3,000 miles away. That is certainly something that could not have been envisaged in Bill Smith's father's time. Bill Smith is astonished at how easily we are seduced into accepting these new innovations.

For example, if you asked passengers on a jetliner, which is basically a thin-skinned rocket flying seven miles above the earth's surface (where the air is so thin it would not keep a mouse alive) well, not one in ten would know what it is that keeps them up there. But those passengers still sit and read a book without a care in the world, as if they are at home in their living room or in the library at Mériadeck (where incidentally, if you know where to go, they have a selection of low-back chairs which are as comfy as deckchairs on a beach and which are ideal for an afternoon snooze). Polly Smith, who is against air travel, says it would serve them right if one of those jetliners simply dropped to the ground like a stone, as it should. That would make it clear, she says, that it is dangerous to take something as preposterous as air travel on blind faith.

After this brief digression, Bill Smith continues with the story.

Our drama begins, as a journalist from *Sud Ouest* might write, in a small settlement up in the northernmost part of the province of Quebec. After that it is Baffin Island and then it is up to the real Arctic and the North Pole and so on.

In the winter the days are short and there are regular snowstorms and howling winds and howling huskies. So everyone gets snuggled down to wait the winter out and it is all very Jack London-like and cosy.

And the Eskimos. Oh no, not Eskimos. They are Inuit now. But why not People of the North? That has bags of romance and dignity. (Things change so quickly it is difficult to keep up. So Bill Smith would like to apologise unreservedly for any offence caused to people with sensitive ears.) But over the winter, whoever they are, they carve primitive sculptures from walrus tusks which are all shipped down and sold to the tourists in Quebec City. (And by the way there is nothing wrong with carving primitive sculptures; it is a very dignified way to make a living, especially from walrus tusks. Have you heard anyone calling out Picasso for painting primitive pictures?)

Bill Smith stops typing and looks out of the window. Are you allowed to carve walrus tusks these days? He is not sure. He thinks about deleting the sentence but decides to let it stay.

And by the way again – and this is relevant – did you see those pictures from the Russian Arctic? The ones that show a pack of fifty polar bears all together, thrusting their snouts into a municipal rubbish tip in a snowbound town? The ice is melting so the polars have nowhere to perch and hunt the seals. So they're starving hungry and have come south in that great big pack in search of food.

So what happens is that a young mother is walking down what is called Rue Principale in the small settlement. She has just picked up her two children from the nearby youth centre. Then suddenly, out of nowhere – he must have been lurking around a corner watching – this big old polar is coming at them, snarling and real fast. He must have been hungry like those Russian polars. And bang, bang, bang! What the old polar does next is he begins to attack the two children. The young mother, once she has got over the shock of seeing a polar on Rue Principale, especially one that is attacking her children just after she has picked them up from the youth centre, well she gets furious so, instead of running away, she stands up to the old polar and begins to attack him back! It is *bam, slam, wham*, if you can believe such a thing. She is giving the old polar a proper biffing. And the old polar is thinking about backing off and calling it a day when an Inuit citizen in a house nearby hears the uproar and comes out with his rifle and shoots the hungry old polar stone dead.

There is even a medical name for what the woman does. It is called 'hysterical strength', which is self-explanatory: in an emergency, people can do amazing things like lift a truck with their bare hands to free someone trapped underneath. Because when there is a battle, hand-to-hand as it were, between a polar and a human being, there should only ever be one winner. But there it is, that is what happened. If Jack London had been around he would certainly have written a story about it. It is that sort of a situation. Anyhow, the upshot is that the two kiddies escape without a scratch but unfortunately the heroic mum has sustained injuries from the claws of the polar and needs immediate medical attention if she is not going to peg out in the next few hours. Hence the urgently arranged medical evacuation flight, the one that is now missing.

Bill Smith stops typing. It has taken longer than expected to get it all down. And there is still Elizabeth and the Grave Constitutional Crisis story to develop, not forgetting those two villainous young lawyers.

So then he yawns and looks at his watch and is surprised to see how late it is. He is beginning to think about a nice mug of hot cocoa before he goes to his bed when Polly Smith pops her head round the door and says, 'Did you hear – I'm sure you didn't because your head was beginning to drop – that there is a love interest developing in the downed Canadian flyer story?'

Sleepy old Bill Smith lifts his head and Polly Smith adds, 'There is an English nurse up there in that settlement as well and she has a soft spot for our pilot, who turns out to be a handsome new immigrant from Norway.'

It seems our story is gathering pace as it goes.

CHAPTER FOUR

The next morning, Bill Smith is brushing his teeth when he realises that to give his narrative credibility he will have to explain why Roger the Diplomat, the confidant of our sovereign, has such an interest in Japan.

As he puts the cap back on the toothpaste, it occurs to him that he has no idea what life in Japan is like. Cherry blossom? People living in houses with walls made of paper? Saki? Mount Fuji and the hunting of whales? It does not amount to much. He has no idea if life in Japan is better or worse than life in England or France. In the end, as he settles in front of the old Underwood to start work, he decides it is probably worse, though he isn't sure why. After a short pause, Bill Smith has one of those brainwaves we all have on occasion and he starts typing.

Among those in the know, certainly those who move in diplomatic circles in Tokyo, Roger is described as having 'done a Chirac'. This is a reference to President Jacques Chirac, our greatly esteemed former president, who now, sadly, is no more. After eating one too many of his favourite dinners of calves' brains, he got the dreaded dementia, which meant in his final years he could no longer tell the Pope from a pint of beer. Long before that, in his early political days as Mayor of Paris, he was known as Le Bulldozer. This is because he had the reputation of a man who gets things done. But what set off Le Tongue Waggers was his strange interest in the faraway country of Japan. Beginning in 1970, Le Bulldozer made more than forty visits to Japan, some private, some official. Eventually, a scandal sheet called *L'Investigateur*, based in Luxembourg of all places, posited the theory that there was what is called a 'love child'. After that it became a free-for-all with candidates for position of mother and offspring offered up and then discarded.

Much amusement was had at the imagined reaction of Chirac's wife, Bernadette, to the news. She was well known for her sanctimony, so she must have driven poor Jacques to, well, driven him to Japan, Bill Smith supposes. (Actually what Jacques Chirac got up to in Paris, never mind Japan, would have made even a saint's hair curl.)

And so, Bill Smith types with a smile, Elizabeth – who is normally so discreet – cannot resist referring, with that delicate laugh which Roger has always found so seductive, to Roger's *'petit problème Chirac'*. Certainly Roger is tempted to bring young Haiku with him next time he is over in England. He is sure Elizabeth will enjoy meeting him.

Bill Smith looks back through the pages written so far and frowns. He mustn't let the two lawyers slip away. He also has to get back to the story of Elizabeth and the Grave Constitutional Crisis. But for the moment he continues with the story of Bill and Polly Smith who, in the cool of the evening, are sipping post-supper digestives on the terrace of the Café Français opposite the cathedral on Place Pey-Berland. They are still chewing over that strange tale of Goya's missing head. Bill Smith is wondering about Dr G and the note he left.

'Why on earth would you leave an explanatory note in a coffin?'

He turns to Polly Smith. Polly Smith replies that he must have had a premonition that the body would be exhumed.

'Guilty conscience more like it,' Bill Smith replies and takes up his cognac.

It is then that Polly Smith asks Bill Smith whether he knows the story of the strange perambulations of the body of Michel de Montaigne. To which Bill Smith replies, 'No.'

So, briefly, a little background. Because again, thinking forward and if packaged correctly, there could be something offbeat here that might hook a Hollywood film producer.

Michel de Montaigne, Bordeaux's own home-grown philosopher, died in 1592 leaving behind a collection of essays which, in today's edition, comes in at over 1000 pages, which is obviously too much for any normal person to read. It's like being faced with one of those enormous burgers that you can't get into your mouth so you are forced to attack it with knife and fork. In fact, if you were to drop a modern edition of the essays of Michel de Montaigne on your foot you would certainly need a trip to the hospital. It is that sort of book. But if you are interested you can buy edited versions which contain the best bits. He is 'folksy' and full of good homespun common sense.

For instance, after a brush with death when he fell from his horse he wrote, 'If you don't know how to die, don't worry. Nature will tell you what to do on the spot, fully and adequately. She will do this job perfectly for you. Don't bother your head about it.'

But what draws a circus gal like Polly Smith to Michel de Montaigne is his reputation for playing host to troupes of acrobats and performers at Château de Montaigne, his estate in the Dordogne, thirty miles to the west of Bordeaux. In other words, as well as writing thousands of serious words he was also a bit of a joker and an entertainer. Unfortunately, this did not sit well with his poor wife, Françoise de la Chassaigne, and they ended up living in opposing turrets of the family chateau.

Polly Smith indicates to a waiter to bring two more cognacs.

'Michel de Montaigne dies at the family chateau in 1592, aged 59,' she continues. 'And because he is so well known – he had at one time been a popular mayor of Bordeaux – everyone wants a piece of him. So what the widow Françoise does is order the heart to be cut out and buried in the chapel on the family estate while the rest of the body is sent to Bordeaux to be interred in a specially carved tomb at the Couvent des Feuillants.'

Here Bill Smith leans forward. 'Hold on,' he says. 'That is exactly what happened to the English writer Thomas Hardy. His heart was cut out and sent for burial *en famille* in Dorset, while the rest of him was buried in state in Westminster Abbey.'

Then Bill Smith starts to chuckle. 'There's a story, which is a true one, that the doctor who was cutting out Hardy's heart was called away urgently and when he returned he found the cat on the dissecting table, eating the heart. So what he did was to have the cat killed and put in the casket alongside what remained of the heart.'

Imagine the scene, Bill Smith types. The family is assembled in the small country church in Dorset. And then paraded down the aisle is a casket containing the half-eaten remains of old Tom's heart and beside it a dead cat! It's amazing anyone kept a straight face. Actually, again, if you proposed that as the opening scene of a film to one of those producers of offbeat Hollywood comedies, against all the odds you might just get a bite. And if they can do something as crazy as that, Bill Smith adds, it's only a short step further for the mourners to erect a grill at the back of the church and, under the auspices of the vicar, cook up the heart and divide it into strips. After that everyone in the assembled company can eat a slice in the sincere belief that they will take on some of old Tom's humanity if not his writing ability.

Then Bill Smith thinks of Professor B and his examination of Goya's skull. Had he been tempted to grind the skull into a powder and ingest a small dose of it himself? That is what the Chinese do today with rhino horn – though whether that makes them great lovers, great artists or just great idiots is unknown.

It's then that Polly Smith, her patience tried, leans forward across the cafe table to ask if Bill Smith has finished so she can continue her story, to which Bill Smith bows his head in shamed assent.

'So, to cut a long story short,' Polly Smith continues, 'for the next 200 years Montaigne's body lies more or less undisturbed in its elaborately carved tomb at the Couvent des Feuillants. But then along comes the wonderful French Revolution, bringing with it a change of air, etc., etc., and Montaigne is now regarded as the great free thinker. So in 1800 the Bordeaux city authorities announce they're going to move Montaigne's body out of the old convent.'

Bill Smith stops to stretch out his elbows and shoulders and give his fingers a shake before continuing to type, setting the scene he hopes will hook the Hollywood film producers.

'It's a fine spring morning in 1800,' Polly Smith says. 'Colourful crowds line the city streets. Then, in the distance, there's a fanfare of trumpets as gaily dressed soldiers and a marching band appear. Then the great philosopher's carved tomb, drawn on a carriage by four magnificent white horses, passes slowly by on its way to its new resting place in the centre of the city.'

Polly Smith pauses and looks around.

With her rakish hats and her strange eyes, Polly Smith can be quite the tease, quite the imp, when she wants to be. Finally Bill Smith is forced to ask, 'So what's the next scene then?'

This makes Polly Smith laugh out loud.

'Oh come on Bill, you old silly! Can't you guess? It isn't Montaigne in the coffin at all! It's the wife of one of his nephews, a woman named Marie de Brian. The clots have only dug up the wrong body! Don't tell me you didn't see that coming?'

Bill Smith looks at her in astonishment. 'I mean, does no one even do a cursory check of these things?' he asks. But Polly Smith is already continuing with her story.

'When the mistake is discovered it's all hushed up. Marie de Brian is quietly removed, but this time without benefit of marching bands and gaily dressed soldiers. And Montaigne stays in his carved tomb at the convent, now converted into a school.'

By this time Bill Smith has paid the bill at the Café Français and they have crossed the square and are walking arm in arm down the Rue du Loup. As they approach the apartment, Polly Smith takes the key from her pocket to open the door.

'The next thing that happens is that there's a fire at the school,' she is saying. 'Montaigne's elaborate carved tomb is left keeled over. The coffin inside is also open to the elements. So eventually the whole ensemble – coffin, bones and carved tomb – is trundled up to the Chartreuse Cemetery. Date about 1880.'

They are now sitting at the kitchen table. Bill Smith, who had been thinking of a cup of cocoa before they go to bed, suddenly looks up at Polly.

'Hold on,' he says. 'That means Montaigne and Goya find themselves in the Chartreuse Cemetery at the same time.'

Polly Smith laughs and hands Bill Smith his cup of cocoa.

'Well it is the main cemetery in the city.' She pauses. 'But there is something else.'

Bill Smith looks up.

'When the carved tomb arrives at the cemetery, the gravediggers take the bones out of the coffin and put them into storage. Then a few years later – 1886 to be exact – the bones are taken back out of storage and put into a nice new oak coffin. You could stretch a point and call it an exhumation.'

Bill Smith puts down his mug of cocoa.

'Then the whole ensemble – the restored carved tomb and the new coffin – is trundled back down to what is now the Musée d'Aquitaine. It's still there today. You can stand in front of it to pay your respects to the great man if you want,' Polly Smith says. 'A lot of people do.'

Bill Smith starts to laugh. He ticks off the points on his fingers.

'Goya and Montaigne, the artist and the philosopher, live in different countries in different centuries. But they both end up at the Chartreuse Cemetery in Bordeaux. And they're both minus body parts. Goya the head, Montaigne the heart. Then in 1888 Goya is exhumed and taken back to Spain. And now you are telling me that Montaigne is also exhumed and removed from the same cemetery just two years earlier?'

In other words, Dear Reader, Bill Smith types, we are up against dear old Carl Jung and his theory of synchronicity once more. (Not to mention that Goya and Montaigne entered this story entirely separately with no intention on the part of the writer that they should ever meet.)

Polly Smith puts the cups into the sink. Then she turns back to Bill Smith.

'Actually, we aren't finished yet.'

They walk through to the bedroom as she continues, 'I wonder if you know that a couple of years ago the Musée d'Aquitaine got a new director?'

Not waiting for an answer, she turns down the cover of the bed.

'Anyway, what this new director does one fine morning is to go poking around in the basement. And what he finds is a blocked-up storage space in a wall.'

Bill Smith is listening carefully.

'So the new director asks around but no one remembers that storage space ever being opened. Well, to cut another long story short, after a lot of backwards and forwards the director orders in a specialist archaeological team to check out what's in the storage space.'

Bill Smith has finished brushing his teeth and is listening intently.

'When they open up the storage space what they discover inside, to gasps of astonishment all round, is a well-made oak coffin with the name Montaigne printed neatly on the side.'

Bill Smith starts to laugh.

'So you mean people have been paying their respects in front of an empty tomb! The old joker has been hiding in the basement all along!'

'Exactly,' says Polly Smith. 'When it is finally all sorted out *Sud Ouest* will certainly have an article entitled 'The Incredible Perambulations of the Body of Michel de Montaigne', next to a story headlined 'Has Anyone Seen Goya's Skull?''

'And the Hollywood film producers will certainly call the Montaigne film *The Wrong Box*,' Bill Smith adds as he buttons up his pyjamas.

'Oh, and I forgot to say; they found something else in the storage space.'

Bill Smith looks around.

'You don't mean …?'

'Yep, I certainly do. Next to the coffin in the storage space what they find is a well-preserved skull.'

'Well I never,' says Bill Smith.

The next day, as there are no cruise ships tied up at the Quais, Bill and Polly Smith decide, following their discussion of the night before, to take a trip to the Musée d'Aquitaine to see Montaigne's carved tomb for themselves. (And by the way, even if you are not interested in such things, you can take it on trust from people who know that in the philosophical world Michel de Montaigne is still a seriously big noise.)

So now Bill and Polly Smith are in the museum, which is only a five-minute walk from their apartment, and they are standing in front of the stone tomb with its carved representation of Montaigne. He is all kitted out in his armour and so on and they are thinking how solid and well carved it is and all that. They are also having a chuckle at all the visitors who have admired the tomb imagining they are in close proximity to the great philosopher when all along he is below their feet in the basement.

It is then that they see, to their surprise, a sign for an exhibition in another part of the museum, for the adventures of Jack London. But this time the adventure is not in the snowy north. This time Jack London is making a voyage to the South Seas on board his sailing ship, the *Snark*. So, deciding they have had enough of old Montaigne – for all his sociability when alive there is only so long you can look at an empty stone tomb – they decide to take in the Jack London exhibition.

And of course it is once again quite the coincidence because Bill Smith's father read all the Jack London stories when he was in his mining camp in Northern Quebec. And right now Bill and Polly Smith are following the story of the downed Norwegian Flyer and the Inuit lady who was attacked by the old polar. As Bill Smith says, that is surely a story that would have had Jack London reaching for his pen.

Time and space allowing, Bill Smith will recount Jack London's adventures in the South Seas. He visited the island of Nuku Hiva in the Marquesas, which Herman Melville had written about sixty-five years before. In one of the valleys on the island, so Melville said, there was a village where people lived in a prelapsarian harmony, while also practising cannibalism. So that is more heads and other body parts missing!

Anyhow, they are coming towards the end of the exhibition, which has absorbed them, when for some reason Bill Smith glances out of the corner of his eye. And this makes him do a double take. Because what he sees behind them and across the other side of the room are the two lawyers he had overheard on the tram planning the murder.

They are dressed more casually and without their attaché cases, but it is certainly them. They are heads down and attentive to the exhibition. So he whispers a warning into Polly Smith's ear and she looks alarmed. He signals to her not to say anything but to move casually towards the exit. But as they are leaving the lawyers walk past them and the smaller one, the one Bill Smith calls the Fox, catches his eye and once again Bill Smith knows he has been clocked.

That night when they get home Bill and Polly Smith try to figure out the chances that it was coincidence. In the end they cannot dismiss the possibility that they are being followed. In other words, they had better watch themselves. Polly Smith says as they are going to bed that night, 'I hope it is not our murder they are planning,' which makes Bill Smith think for a long time before he finally drops off to sleep.

CHAPTER FIVE

Bill Smith stops typing and taps his pencil against the side of the typewriter. Where to go next? Stick with the lawyers in the Musée d'Aquitaine? Follow Jack London to San Francisco as he fits out the *Snark* for his voyage to the South Seas? In the end he opts for Elizabeth and Roger the Diplomat and sets to work.

There is a note from Elizabeth waiting for Roger in his rooms when he returns from Japan. As Elizabeth expects old friends to be as well-informed as ministers, Roger spends the next two days getting up to speed on the news before driving up to Sandringham.

It's six months since their last meeting. Elizabeth looks tired. She has no confidence in Charles so she still keeps up a punishing schedule – and of course Philip's health has been a worry for some time.

You could say, in fact, that Philip has always been a worry. Everyone knows about the fairy-tale marriage in 1947. But Roger's impression, having seen them together over the years, is that the relationship went rather on the frosty side early on. We will come back to the reasons for this later on, time and space allowing.

So now Roger is telling Elizabeth that, while Haiku is settling into a new school and getting satisfactory reports, the mood in Tokyo is subdued. Elections and a new government are anticipated and the feeling is that it will not end well.

Then Elizabeth pours the tea and leans forward.

It is at this critical moment in the narrative that Polly Smith pops her head round the door to say that a house does not run itself and that there are dishes to be washed and beds to be made, etc. Then she exits abruptly in a manner which might be described as 'with a rumble of thunder'. This interruption leaves Bill Smith looking blankly at his typewriter, the next scene gone clean out of his mind.

To backtrack and explain all that, both Bill and Polly Smith have been shaken up by the encounter with the two lawyers the previous day. They are unsure whether it is a coincidence in the Carl Jung sense or something more sinister, i.e. they have been put under surveillance by the lawyers. The strange story of the missing plane in Northern Quebec and the poor Inuit lady who has been savaged by the polar bear is also giving them pause for reflection on the fragility of life. So it is perhaps unsurprising, on the basis of upsetting news coming in twos or threes or whatever it is, that this morning he should have had a slight tiff with Polly Smith.

In the great scheme of life it is nothing very much. It is actually down to incorrect use of a towel in the bathroom. Polly Smith is fussy about things like that. She also dislikes the cap not being put back on the toothpaste. Cupboard doors left open are a real killer for her.

When Bill Smith had queried this attitude and said that it did not seem to be on a level with the bohemian life of a circus performer, Polly Smith had given him a withering look and said if you were a high-wire walker and if you did not perfect your sense of balance – or if, to put it in Bill Smith's words, you were bohemian about your security arrangements – you would not last long.

So Bill Smith, as he does on these occasions, puts his typewriter to one side and goes out for a stroll and to buy that morning's edition of *Sud Ouest*, in which, Dear Reader – and here is a bit of a tease – he will find some interesting news. He also goes to the nearby Patisserie Solaris to buy a nice little cake for after their lunch as a form of 'making up.'

His visit to Patisserie Solaris will also allow him to engage in a little flirtatious chit-chat with Gloria who works behind the counter. She is originally from El Salvador and has a smile that warms Bill Smith's heart, though he is wise enough not to mention this to Polly Smith. So he is disappointed when the Chinese lady who owns Patisserie Solaris, and whom everyone calls either Madame Chopsticks or The Dragon Lady, serves him herself, saying that Gloria has not come into work that morning.

Which is of course a clue he should have picked up on.

Aside from the occasional tiff, which is normal, Bill and Polly Smith live in a domestic harmony which would be the envy of most couples. They are also, for all the eccentricities of Polly Smith and their surprising way of making a living, quite a traditional couple.

Every Saturday morning for instance, when there are no cruise boats in, they go to the market at Capucins near the Place de la Victoire where they buy carefully selected vegetables and fruit for the week. It is a moment to anticipate when the first strawberries appear in May, followed by the first melons in June. In winter they feast on apples and pears and Polly Smith makes delicious vegetable soups. When they have finished their shopping they often stop to have their lunch at one of the little eateries in the market where, during the season, you can get very reasonably priced oysters.

Bill Smith also takes his turn in the kitchen. He makes a pizza with anchovies and olives that is not bad at all and his tagine, which he makes once a week over the winter, is – whisper it not – better than many of the tagines the Moroccan restaurants in the city offer. He also washes the dishes and puts out the bins, etc. In other words, as much as a man can, he does his bit. Polly Smith is in charge of the more intimate arrangements such as making the bed and arranging clothes and so on.

Bill Smith also considers he has something of an aptitude as a bread maker. His specialty is a type of olive bread for which he has invented his own recipe. His secret, he says, is to add plenty of the good-quality olives he buys in the market. If the day is warm, he puts the dough out on the balcony to let it rise. Bill Smith bakes his olive bread at 200 degrees for 55 minutes. Polly Smith always says that it tastes delicious.

However, neither Bill Smith nor Polly Smith bake cakes because the excellent Patisserie Solaris is just around the corner from their apartment.

When they entertain it is usually for Polly Smith's extended family of circus performers. Bill Smith says that despite their slim builds they have voracious appetites. Polly Smith prepares a duck stuffed with olives while Bill Smith sees to the canapes and the wine. They generally serve a Madiran from the Gers which, as noted in an earlier chapter, can be a considered a peculiar preference. When asked about it, Bill Smith says while on their honeymoon bicycling in the Gers they had arrived one evening at an auberge in a small village. They were still wet through after a late-afternoon downpour and were tired and hungry. When they finally came down to dinner, the owner of the auberge produced from her cellar a bottle of Madiran which they both agreed was the best wine they had ever drunk. They had noted the estate and, through a wine merchant in the city, they had sourced a supply which they now use for family and special occasions.

So there we are. Bill Smith has selected his gateau and it is now nestling in its cardboard box neatly tied with coloured ribbon. It is his peace offering. As he walks back he calls in to the local *tabac* to buy *Sud Ouest*. Polly Smith has all sorts of theories about the owner of the *tabac*, none of them flattering. In fact she calls him a brute. His views come free with the newspaper and you would not say they were enlightened.

So when Bill Smith is back in the apartment, his ears still ringing with the *tabac* owner's latest bilge, he puts the cake down on the table and starts to leaf through the paper. His eye is caught, (I wonder if you saw this one coming, Dear Reader? If you are a reader of detective novels you probably have), by a small news item headed 'Body Found In River'.

It is not Bill Smith's intention to turn this story into a geography lesson but, briefly, the city of Bordeaux sits in a loop on the river River Garonne rather romantically called Port de la Lune. This is where the cruise boats moor up. The city has a magnificent eighteenth-century waterfront with buildings all scrubbed and fresh and clean and looking as pretty as a picture.

But it's the river we need to focus on here. A first impression is that it is wide and brown: a slow-moving, lazy old river. This is deceptive. Even though Bordeaux is eighty miles from the sea, the river is still fiercely tidal as it passes through the city. There is also the flow of water coming down from headwaters up country. So if you were to stand on the Pont de Pierre and look over the parapet you would be surprised at the swirling current and the speed of the river. Certainly if you tumbled into the Garonne from any of the bridges that span it you'd have to be a strong swimmer to reach the bank.

The girl, the report in *Sud Ouest* says, has been identified as coming from Marseille, which incidentally is Polly Smith's home town. She is described as 'slim build, early 20s with hair in a pony tail', so Bill Smith says straightaway that she must be a student. The body was spotted by passers-by, close to the bank up by the new concert hall at Floirac which, to give you a location, is on the right bank upstream of the Pont de Pierre.

Bill Smith is reading the report aloud to Polly Smith at the kitchen table.

'Described as happy-go-lucky, circle of friends, close family, no history of depression, etc.' His eyes move down the column of newsprint. 'Doesn't sound like a jumper at all.'

Then Bill Smith says, 'Aha!' and Polly Smith looks up. He touches the article with his finger.

'Now this is where it gets interesting.'

Bill Smith points to a rather fuzzy picture of what appears to be a search party poking about in the rushes on the right bank. They are downstream of the Pont de Pierre and opposite the Place de la Bourse.

Bill Smith looks up and says to Polly Smith, 'They're searching near the club. You know, the outdoor place where they play music, it runs down to the river. We've been there. She must have told a friend that's where she was going.'

Suddenly Bill Smith stands up. 'She went with the lawyers. They got her drunk and pushed her into the river and drowned her. That's what happened. I'm sure of it.'

Polly Smith says as a theory it is interesting but she can't go further than that.

After that Bill and Polly Smith have to look a bit lively and get their outfits ready as an American cruise ship is due to come up the river and moor at the Quais that afternoon. It is only later that evening that Bill Smith is able to return to the scene at Sandringham, where Elizabeth has just poured the tea.

Roger is certain that Elizabeth will return to the Bob Boothby story, Bill Smith types. The Queen Mother always described Boothby as 'a bounder but not a cad'. This is a phrase that makes Roger laugh.

Instead, Elizabeth takes a sip of her tea and says, 'I was thinking about the times he came to Balmoral,' and Roger realises that Elizabeth is referring not to Bob Boothby but to Harold Macmillan.

Bill Smith stops typing and taps his pencil against the side of the typewriter. It's going to be the devil of a job to get all this down. He sighs. But there is background that has to be established. Without this background it will be impossible to understand Elizabeth's actions which, as stated in the first chapter of this account, gave rise to the danger of that Grave Constitutional Crisis. Bill Smith pauses and then realises that the only thing he can do is take a run at it and hope the readers will follow.

The three principal actors are: Harold Macmillan, his wife Dorothy and Lord 'Bob' Boothby. Actually, there is also a fourth already introduced, i.e. Elizabeth's husband, Philip.

First out of the traps is Harold Macmillan: Eton and Oxford; shrapnel wounded in WW1 and prime minister (Conservative) from 1957 to 1963. Can be referred to as an old-style Edwardian gent, aware of duties and obligations and so on. He has a droopy face and a droopy moustache, all of which gives him, when he is older, a rather 'arf-arf' seal-like look. He has old-fashioned manners and courtesies, for example always dressing for dinner in black tie. He also has that archaic way of speaking. For instance, he uses four syllables to pronounce the word parliament. Try it. You will get the idea. It is said that he covers up a latent shyness by being a performer, a bit of a card. Others of his contemporaries call him a bore because he tends to lecture. Still others laugh at him because he shuffles slightly as he walks, due to his shrapnel war wound. Actually, he is pretty damn clever and pretty damn sharp. He is affectionately known, at least by a section of the public, as 'Supermac'. The newspapers also call him a One Nation Tory, which means that providing the working class mind their Ps and Qs and don't get too rowdy he will do his damnedest to look after them. Which, actually, you could say is not a bad way of governing a country. But the key word to remember with Harold Macmillan is melancholy, the reason for which will soon become clear.

Next up for examination is Macmillan's wife, Dorothy. They marry in 1920 and stay married for 46 years until she dies in 1966. She likes to be known as Lady Dorothy. And oh my goodness, Bill Smith types, what a bill of goods is she. She has been described as being really quite ugly but at the same time having great sexual attraction. Which is an interesting combination, Bill Smith adds.

Dorothy Macmillan is of Cavendish stock, from that family known as the Devonshires. In case you do not follow these things, the Cavendishes or Devonshires are one of the grand families of old England. The family seat is Chatsworth House, Derbyshire. Some say they are even grander than the Mountbatten-Windsors. But so often is the word 'bloody' attached as an adjective to the Cavendish family that one could be forgiven for thinking, Bill Smith types, that they are actually called the Bloody-Cavendishes. Their other family trait is alcoholism. Sometimes you have to be blunt about these things and just say it the way it is.

So now finally, Dear Reader, let us with a roll of the drums and a tinkle on the trumpet enter into the court docket the pantomime villain of the piece, Robert John Graham Boothby or, to give him his full moniker, Baron Boothby of Buchan and Rattray Head, known to his friends as Bob, and candidate for the most corrupt personage of this modern era. But you must always remember that the word 'corrupt' can also encompass the words 'charming', 'witty' and 'seductive'. If you were going to be a literary fancy pants you could probably use the word 'effulgent' to describe Bob Boothby and get away with it.

Here is a shorthand character outline for Bob Boothby: enlightened politician, even conscience of his generation, but always getting into scrapes. Alley cat morals but has the real common touch. The people love him. They call him 'Bob Boothby, the old rogue.'

But to get back to our story and the reason for Harold's melancholy, what happens is that in the 1920s Bob Boothby and Harold Macmillan are both young backbench Tory MPs. They are close, both politically and personally. Then, out of the blue on a shooting holiday in Scotland in 1929, Boothby takes it into his head to seduce Harold's wife, Dorothy. Astonishingly, the subsequent affair then runs, on and off, for the next thirty years. And the bad bit is that Boothby and Dorothy Macmillan make no effort to hide their affair; they flaunt themselves in public and Harold is left completely humiliated. But Harold refuses Dorothy's request for a divorce because in spite of everything, he tells friends, he is still deeply in love with her. So they continue to share the marital home – though living at opposite ends of the building. One thinks of Michel de Montaigne and his wife Françoise living in opposing turrets of the family chateau.

The newspapers are more deferential in those days so nothing appears in print but, in private, there is a lot of damaging talk. As a result, all the Macmillan children go off the rails. They have terrible troubles with alcohol and the youngest, Sarah, is never sure who is her papa: Boothby or Macmillan.

Elizabeth and her mother and the rest of the royal household watch the whole awful drama unfold. Elizabeth is of a generation younger but she is still sensible of the situation. She was close to her father, King George, so she is at ease in the company of older men. Naturally, therefore, she is for Harold and against Dorothy and Bob Boothby.

So now to return briefly to that afternoon tea at Sandringham, before wrapping up this segment.

'You know, of course, the Cavendishes were horrible to Harold right from the beginning?' Elizabeth is leaning forward over the tea things to make her point. 'When he and Dorothy went to lunch at Chatsworth, before they were married, they had a competition to see who could avoid sitting next to Harold at lunch. They said he was a bore and that he had funny teeth and that he used to lecture. They laughed at him behind his back. Harold was terribly upset.'

Bill Smith stops typing. There are certain points he needs to clarify, especially in relation to Harold and Elizabeth, but just then Polly Smith calls out from the bedroom to ask if he plans to stay up all night.

Bill Smith glances at his watch and is surprised to see how late it is. He quickly wraps up the chapter.

Among the supporting cast still to appear in this aristocratic drama are: Ronnie and Reggie Kray, two of the most vicious East End criminals you could ever come across; Dorothy Macmillan's brother, Edward Cavendish; and John Bodkin Adams, a Northern Irish doctor who can lay title to being the most prolific serial killer in British history.

So that is something to look forward to!

CHAPTER SIX

If ever there were a vacancy for a juggler in Polly Smith's circus Bill Smith would certainly get the part. He is currently trying to keep in the air all the main strands of this story: the lawyers full of murderous intent, the complicated lives of the English aristocracy, the adventures of Jack London, the perambulations of the bodies of Goya and Montaigne and not forgetting the search for the downed plane in the Canadian North.

So now Bill and Polly Smith are sitting at their usual table at the Café Français enjoying a glass of wine in the cool of the evening. Polly Smith is recapitulating on the love angle in the downed flyer story in the Canadian North.

'The flyer,' she is saying, 'is a handsome young immigrant from Norway, while the English nurse is turning out to be quite the English Rose.'

Bill Smith nods. That's background; he knows that.

Polly Smith tips back her colourful straw hat.

'So what if we say that the English Rose is now up in one of the giant search aircraft herself?'

'Oh, that's not bad,' Bill Smith replies with a smile.

Bill Smith stops typing and closes his eyes, the better to imagine the scene in his head. Finally he opens his eyes again and begins to type.

The giant plane, he writes, has been up in the air an hour before it reaches the search area. The pilot, under instruction from a grizzled old loadmaster, is now lowering a cargo ramp underneath the belly of the plane. Then he is slowing the plane right down and they're going in at a low height.

At the same time the courageous English Rose is layering up in every piece of clothing she can find before adding hat, gloves, goggles, etc. Then she is inching her way out onto the ramp before being strapped in place by the grizzled old loadmaster and two other crew members.

So now the English Rose is flat out with just her head peering over the edge of the ramp. She is gazing intently down as the search plane passes low over the stumpy forests and frozen lakes. The English Rose is straining every nerve for a glimpse of the downed plane and her beloved Norwegian Flyer.

But because this is such a cold operation it can only be endured for a short time. So after fifteen minutes the disappointed, but not discouraged, English Rose is hauled back from the ramp and thawed out and replaced by another searcher.

Polly Smith is certain that this is an indication of the real love of the English Rose for the Norwegian Flyer. It's also an indication, she adds, that those English Rose types, who come out seeking adventure in the Canadian North, are quite the tough cookies.

Bill Smith wonders in a light-hearted sort of way – though of course he does not voice this thought – whether the English Rose may also be wanting to make sure that her Norwegian Flyer is not going *jug, jug, jug,* in a nice warm sleeping bag with the Inuit lady.

Anyway, at the end of the story Polly Smith is looking at Bill Smith with a quizzical eye while at the same time fiddling with the stem of her wine glass. She is asking herself whether Bill

Smith would dangle from the underside of a plane in sub-zero temperatures in a search for her.

Bill Smith notices the look on Polly Smith's face. It makes him move uneasily in his seat so he signals to the waiter for two more glasses of wine before commenting airily that 'the cruise boats are now so big you wonder how they ever get up the river at all'.

Bill Smith stops typing.

Bill Smith would love to describe Polly Smith as a 'flamboyant circus performer with long, flowing scarf and tilted straw hat and different-coloured eyes that are at the same time both seductive and angelic'. But nowadays you need to box clever over that sort of thing. Sexism is a serious charge for a writer to be brought up on; along with cultural appropriation it's a really bad thing to do. Charges in either of those categories can be a career-ending situation.

There are also question marks over a writer having a sense of humour. A lot of publishers are counselling writers to 'cut out the jokes' in case they offend.

In the end Bill Smith decides to take a chance and call Polly Smith 'flamboyantly brilliant' and hope that no offence is taken.

Bill Smith stops typing and frowns. The narrative has got out of sequence. For the next scene he needs to take a step back.

So the Norwegian Flyer is on the airstrip at the settlement. He has studied the weather reports and knows a storm is moving in from the east. He glances down at his watch with a worried look. It's already past two. So he'll have to do the last part of the journey down to Quebec City in the dark.

And here is the dilemma: he has only been in the Canadian North a few months so he's not yet qualified to fly by instruments. He's only certified to fly in daylight and when he can see the ground. So there's no way he should take the flight. It breaks all the safety rules. And to make matters worse, on the way up from Quebec City the day before he noted problems with both gyrocompass and radio. But there isn't another plane due for a week and the old polar has chewed up the Inuit lady pretty bad. So if he doesn't take the flight she's probably going to die. So everyone is hanging around and not wanting to say anything and hoping that he will take it.

The waiter puts down two more glasses of wine.

The set-up for these small planes up in the Canadian Arctic is different from regular airports, Bill Smith writes. There are no petrol bowsers coming out onto the tarmac to fill you up or anything like that. In fact, our young Norwegian Flyer has been up on the wing himself filling up the plane only half an hour before.

Polly Smith takes up the story.

'Actually, this is what attracts people such as the Norwegian Flyer and the English Rose. This is the type of adventure they come searching for in the Canadian North.'

'Which is all fine and dandy but at the same time it can all go horribly wrong,' Bill Smith adds.

So what the English Rose is doing up there in the Canadian Arctic is travelling from settlement to settlement, teaching Inuit citizens how to look after themselves from the medical point of view and so on. And because there are no roads and the distances between settlements are so vast the English Rose is being transported around by the young Norwegian Flyer.

'So now,' declares the flamboyantly brilliant Polly Smith, 'it's spring time in the Arctic. The brief blossoming of new life and so on. In other words, the young couple are soon in love. In fact, they are as happy as a couple of kids. They fly from settlement to settlement, over the ice and the snow and the forests and the lakes all gouged out by Nature's rough hand

and never finished and never tamed. One day they see a line of migrating caribou and the Norwegian Flyer swoops the plane down low and they shout out, "Woo hoo!" and "Wah hah!".'

So this is a real Jack London style adventure they are having up in the Canadian North, Bill Smith types.

Over long dinners at night, the Norwegian Flyer tells the English Rose all the stories of the Canadian North, even though he has not been there long and Jack London would certainly say he is 'still wet behind the ears'.

But he has all the confidence of youth. One evening he even tells the English Rose what you have to do if your plane is forced down.

'First,' he says, 'You must turn your plane into a shelter and build a fire and so on. But then – and this is important – you cannot start straightaway on your emergency ration box. Which, incidentally, comes in a cute little case and, if it has been properly maintained, should contain tins of corned beef, packets of soup, dried mashed potato, rice, raisins, powdered eggs, biscuits and tea bags.'

'But hold on,' the English Rose says, watching her handsome Norwegian Flyer. He is shovelling good-sized steaks onto plates. 'Why on earth can't the survivors dive straight into these emergency rations? Surely they could be a lifesaver?'

So the Norwegian Flyer says with a smile, as he opens a bottle of wine, 'Well, figure it out. The bit of the Canadian Arctic you have landed in is the size of France with only a few grumpy old polars and a few grumpy old Inuit seal hunters, so it could be a long time before you are spotted and rescued.

'So what the experts recommend,' the handsome Norwegian Flyer says as they tuck into their steaks, 'is to eat as little as possible to begin with. But so you don't feel hungry you first have to shrink your stomach. And to do this – it's the recommendation of all the survival experts – you must eat nothing at all for the first two days.'

As you can imagine, Bill Smith types, this is a surprise to the English Rose.

But once he is on a roll, and with that confidence of youth, there is no stopping the Norwegian Flyer. So as he puts desserts on the table he continues, 'Even after two days, the experts say, you must still not start on your rations in their cute little case. What you must first do is to take the fishing line and fishing hooks that come in your survival pack and find a lake or open water or stream or river and fish, fish, fish, for all your life's worth and you can also lay traps to catch rabbits and so on, which you can roast over your fire in the evening like the gypsies used to do, only they used to do it with hedgehogs. It is only when all this is done and you have exhausted everything else and you are exhausted yourself and the stubble on the chin is turning into beard and it is all getting a bit hard going that you can start to nibble at your rations.

'And that is the way,' the handsome Norwegian Flyer says as he opens a box of chocolate mints and serves the coffee, 'that providing you drink two pints of water a day, which is no problem with all the snow around you, you can survive at least sixty days.'

And to complete this anecdote and show its usefulness or 'relevance', Bill Smith types, you will certainly know someone who intends to fly over the Canadian Arctic within the next couple of weeks – or at least you would have done, before the Great Plague – because many of the jet liners use that route to the New World. So in that case you had better get right on the telephone to your friend who is going to take that trip and warn them, in case they are downed, not to start on their emergency rations straightaway but to starve themselves for two days! So we can now return once again to that scene at the airstrip.

The young Norwegian Flyer is still hesitating. He is weighing up the dangers. He is concerned about the radio and the gyrocompass. The handful of people on the airstrip, including the English Rose and of course the family of the injured Inuit lady, are all watching him.

Finally he snaps out of it and says, his English still with a pronounced Nordic accent, 'Okay lets go; let's get the plane loaded.' Then the tension winds down and the Inuit lady gets loaded carefully into the plane and people start to drift away until finally only the English Rose is left.

Now the Norwegian Flyer is in the cockpit checking the controls when the English Rose steps forward and hands him a packet of sandwiches and a Thermos of coffee and in a voice loaded up with love says, 'Bon voyage mon amour.'

The next scene is the English Rose standing on the airstrip, watching the small plane, piloted by her handsome Norwegian Flyer, take off into the darkening sky. Certainly Jack London would have made a story out of that last, lingering look up.

As she walks away, the heart of the English Rose is heavy with foreboding. And this foreboding is heightened by a report from a local journalist, broadcast shortly after take off. He is one of those bushy-tailed young reporters, Bill Smith types, all vim and vigour and with a good dose of loose morals. When they smell a story that can make their reputation they get excited. It is like catnip to them.

What the reporter has discovered is that one of the pivotal ground beacons the Norwegian Flyer will use to orient himself on his way down to Quebec City is not working.

'Probably stepped on by a goddamn caribou,' Polly Smith says grimly.

This is actually a serious blow because the Norwegian Flyer, in making his decision, had calculated that he could always follow the radio beacons on the ground and they would orient him.

The reporter then gets into a long discussion with another pilot about gyrocompasses and magnetic deviation up there in the Canadian North.

This makes Bill Smith think of Jack London and his adventures in the South Seas, where he also faced great navigational problems – which we will come to later, time and space allowing.

By the way, Dear Reader, here is a little deviation for you. Did you know that when he went on his voyage to the South Seas, Jack London took a gramophone and a series of records with him and that the playlist is still available? The islanders are said to have clapped and danced to the songs.

Bill Smith stops and taps the side of the typewriter with his pencil and considers how to proceed. Finally he makes a decision and starts once again.

The Inuit lady is wrapped up in blankets behind the pilot's seat. The Norwegian Flyer can hear her regular breathing, so that is reassuring. He checks that they're on the correct heading that will take them down to Quebec City then he opens the packet of sandwiches. Lunch is something he had not thought about before setting off.

The English Rose has written a love note in her pretty round hand and tucked it into the sandwich packet. The Norwegian Flyer looks out at the rugged Arctic landscape below him and imagines their future together. He whistles a tune and thinks he must be the luckiest person alive.

There is the first indication of trouble when the rising wind gives the plane a warning bump. The Norwegian Flyer glances uneasily to the east and sees the sky is already darkening. So the big old storm is approaching. He's going to lose the light and need to fly by instruments earlier than anticipated. Then the rising wind bumps the plane again and the Inuit lady behind him groans out loud. All this gives him a queer feeling in his tummy.

He tries to calm himself. Out loud he says, 'Well at least the sky is still bright to the west.' He looks anxiously around. Then the gyrocompass is suddenly all over the place and then he can't raise anyone on the radio. Then he misses the homing beacon which will give him his position. The wind gives his plane another bump, which is much rougher than the others. When he looks down again the ground has disappeared altogether, which gives him that queer feeling in his tummy again.

And now we come to something that even Jack London never knew about.

We know that the sky is rapidly darkening from the east and that the wind is rising and the storm is approaching. But to the west the sky is still clear. The sun is dipping low but for the moment it's still above the horizon. Experienced pilots know about this phenomenon. They know that in moments of danger like this they will be drawn, almost magnetically, to the warmth and life of the sun. So they eye the compass to make sure they stay on their correct bearing.

But our young Norwegian Flyer is ignorant of all that and is drifting ever further west, desperate to hang on to that dipping sun. And so in a few minutes he is way off course and when the sun finally does drop down below the horizon he is in all sorts of trouble; the compass is swinging wildly, visibility is zero and the storm is increasing in force. He tries the radio but still nothing. So in fact he is pretty much lost.

The plane is being pushed violently from side to side. In the back the Inuit lady is groaning out loud. The flyer clicks on the cabin light and opens out the map on his knees. Then his heart gives a jump because he spots a river marked on the map. If he can dip down under the clouds he can find the river and follow it.

So he dips the plane down. But he hasn't realised how far west he has drifted and that he's actually over a raised plateau. And by the time he realises his error he is skimming the tree tops and it's too late. There's the first unexpected crack and after that it all happens so quickly. They're ploughing through trees and being catapulted nose over tail. It is all horribly violent and loud. And then suddenly it stops and there is a deathly silence and a creeping sense of the cold.

Bill Smith stops typing and looks over the finished pages. He taps the pencil against the side of the typewriter. 'Not Jack London of course,' he says quietly to himself, 'but not bad all the same.'

CHAPTER SEVEN

So here is a puzzle, Dear Reader: what is it that Elizabeth (our sovereign) and Polly Smith (a quayside photographer in Bordeaux) have in common? Answer: they are both great readers of American detective stories. Polly Smith always has two or three on the go from the library at Mériadeck and Roger generally glimpses a Raymond Chandler or an Elmore Leonard by the side of Elizabeth's chair when they are taking tea at Balmoral or Sandringham. This means that both of them can, on occasion, slip into that strange American demotic.

So to set a scene. It is breakfast the following morning. Bill and Polly Smith are discussing their next move in the hunt for the killers. It's then that Polly Smith suddenly says, 'I know, let's smoke 'em out down at the courthouse. If they know we are on to them they may make a desperate move.'

So that is how, later that morning, with domestic chores done and the latest cruise ship not expected until early evening, this unlikely pair of private eyes find themselves at the Palais de Justice on the Place de la République. It is about ten minutes' walk from Bill and Polly Smith's apartment; everything is central here.

To enter the courthouse the pair have to mount an eternity of steps past what are called Doric columns. It is all in the neoclassical style, i.e. with the usual Roman and Greek influences, the Parthenon and so on and so on and blah-de-blah.

Inside, the ceilings are thirty feet high and there are marble floors and alcoves and a few more Doric columns. There is a quotation from Michel de Montaigne printed up on the wall. In other words, it is all so heavy with gravitas it sends a shiver down your spine. Everyone is walking around with long faces as if a hanging has been announced. So if you end up being judged here you know you have been a very bad boy or girl indeed.

(There are actually two court complexes in our city here. The other is contemporary and was designed by the Englishman Rogers but no one takes it seriously because from the outside it looks like one of those bouncy castles. There are some who say that Rogers misunderstood his brief, that he did not realise he was designing a courthouse. In other words it lacks gravitas.)

So now you know where you are, Dear Reader. You are, as they say, oriented.

Bill and Polly Smith pull back one of those giant wooden doors to step inside a court room and … This is a job to describe, but I hope you can bear with us, though you can skip a couple of paragraphs if you are in a hurry and your lunch is waiting.

What Bill and Polly Smith have stumbled into is a massive drugs trial! But it is not one of those drugs trials where there is a Mexican mastermind with an outrageous moustache and witnesses giving evidence from behind screens and soldiers in flak jackets armed with machine guns guarding the doorways. It's not like that at all. This is a much smaller, home-grown affair and chaotic in its operation. And to deviate for a second, here is a complaint that will find sympathy with all of a certain age: why oh why do the young not speak more clearly today? When the defendants are replying to the judge or the prosecutor they mumble so much it is difficult to hear.

Anyhow, Bill and Polly Smith are trying to get their bearings, but the whole place is a scrum. Eventually they find a place on the crowded public benches and sit down. They are surrounded by colourfully dressed defendants with tattoos and resplendent hairstyles. At first glance it is difficult to know who are defendants and who are supporting family and friends. People are laughing and shuffling about and whispering behind their hands. Bill and Polly Smith have the strong impression that they are the only ones present without a criminal record.

To the side of the court there are a dozen lawyers. Bill Smith supposes they are appearing for the various defendants. They spot among them the two young lawyers, so they have picked right.

It is then that Bill Smith goes 'tum-te-tum' and nods his head and mutters under his breath to Polly Smith that they have been clocked by the one they call the Fox.

Bill Smith watches as the Fox taps the Boy on the shoulder and nods towards them. But Bill and Polly Smith are not hiding their presence. This is part of their new strategy. As Polly Smith has said, they are in the courthouse in a bid to 'smoke out' the lawyers.

Their attention then moves to the judge. He has a jowly face with a bristly beard. Bill Smith guesses that he is between fifty and sixty. He looks to have the build of a rugby player, one of those front-row forwards who is all thick neck and rounded shoulders. They watch him hunkered down on his raised bench at the front of the court. After a few minutes' observation, Bill and Polly Smith can see that he has what is called 'a rat-like cunning'. He gives the mob half a yard and makes them laugh then the next minute he reins them in. Anyone can see that despite his looks he is a smart cookie. He encourages one defendant and then slaps down the next. It's the same trick with the lawyers. He charms a female lawyer and then rebuffs an older man. So he is keeping everyone on edge.

After half an hour Bill and Polly Smith pick up the rhythm of the trial. The judge calls up the colourfully clothed defendants, either singly or occasionally in pairs. They stand in front of the microphone in the well of the court to answer his questions. There are additional questions from the prosecutor and occasional interventions from defence lawyers before they return to the benches and the next defendants are called up. The drug ring centres round the Place de la Victoire, and the levels of organisation, with multiple agents and sub-agents, would do any regular enterprise proud. But minds do tend to drift and soon Bill Smith is thinking about other things.

By the way, has it been mentioned yet that, on occasion, Bill Smith has some real bad dreams? Polly Smith calls them his 'yips'. It would be a puzzle even to Carl Jung or any of the other dream merchants as to why these bad dreams should happen, as Bill Smith has never suffered any traumatic occurrence. His life, at least up until now, has tended to the sedentary and predictable and comfortable. Polly Smith considers that this may be the root of the problem. Bill Smith has tended to live his great adventures from afar, i.e. in the books at the library in Mériadeck. So, for instance, he has never been to the Canadian North or photographed a black leopard in Africa. Of course, it may just be that Bill Smith is temperamentally unsuited to the adventurous life, so when a real-life adventure has presented itself it has played on his nerves.

Anyhow, whatever the reason, he'd had a strange one last night. Polly Smith told him, in the morning, she'd had to jump up pretty quick and shine a lamp into his eyes to stop him howling his bloody head off like a dog that's been kicked in the whatsits. Then she said when he had finally opened his eyes he'd blinked and said, 'Sorry about that, old girl,' before going straight back to sleep.

When Bill Smith has these yips it is generally because he is in confrontation with a large beast such as a bear or a lion or a tiger. It is at the moment when the claws of the beast are about to rip into him that Bill Smith gives his bloody great bellow. Sometimes Bill Smith doesn't remember the detail of the nightmare at all. On other occasions it comes back during the day. This morning it is as they are getting ready to come down to the courthouse that Bill Smith gets a sudden clear recall of last night's dream.

So he says to Polly Smith, with a smile on his face, 'Do you know, last night I dreamt I was being butted up the rear end by a unicorn.'

Now, if Polly Smith had been a regular sort of wife (rather than a circus gal with one eye a different colour from the other and a penchant for colourful hats and long, trailing scarves) and if this had been a regular modern novel, following a stereotype as conventional and rigid as anything Jane Austen could dream up (the only difference being that today's heroine wears ripped jeans and is likely to rush to a disciple of Dr Freud or Dr Jung when anything goes wrong), well she would have put down her coffee cup at this revelation from Bill Smith and she would have said, after a moment's thought, 'Well that probably means …' And then away we go and the next minute Bill Smith is in to see a shady fellow with a twitch, who, when he hears that Bill Smith has dreamt he is being butted up the rear end by a unicorn, will say, 'Oh yes please, I'll have some of that.' Because that is something that a good psychiatrist can string out for years on end. And if he gets enough guys like Bill Smith he will be able to afford that place in Spain he has always wanted. He will even name it Casa Unicorn in grateful thanks to Señor Freud and all the rest of the dream merchants.

But Polly Smith is not a regular sort of a wife, and this is not a regular modern novel. So instead – and this is significant, in an insignificant sort of way, to our understanding of Polly Smith – she says, 'Well, in that case you had better go and see Madame Solaris.'

Now, Madame Solaris is a clairvoyant who operates out of a sixth-floor apartment in a block in the Quartier des Aubiers. At night, kids drive hot-rodded cars around the area and it is not too difficult to buy a couple of grams of this and that in the courtyard in front of the block. In other words, it's not the best part of town. No one knows exactly where Madame Solaris is from, though the accent indicates somewhere 'up north'. In the opinion of Polly Smith, who is a regular visitor, you could do as well to turn over a tarot card with Madame Solaris, who has shown herself to get it right more times than not, as to visit a regular 'trick cyclist'.

And here is the strange thing: we are back to our old friend Carl Jung and his theory of synchronicity because of course the patisserie where Gloria works is called Patisserie Solaris, which is either a meaningful coincidence or not, depending on your point of view.

And to divert back for a moment to that business with the missing plane in the frozen north of Quebec, in the end the case is good for Madame Solaris. This is because Polly tells her that the search parties cannot find the downed plane and that a lot of clairvoyants are now getting in on the act. So Madame Solaris gets out her crystal ball and begins to do her busy-busy stuff and comes out half an hour later with a set of coordinates and a description of a lake with a rock in it and so Polly wires off these details to the search organisers. And when it is all over – though we will not say at the moment how it does conclude

– while all the other clairvoyants are way off and you could have stuck a pin in a map blindfold and done as well, Madame Solaris turns out to be right within fifty miles. So this gets out and there is an article about her in *Sud Ouest* extolling her powers, so the police start to call her when they get stuck on a case and so she is beginning to have some success there and to build a name for herself.

Anyway, that is the end of that deviation because there is a development down at the courthouse.

It happens when a defendant sitting next to Bill and Polly Smith, and dressed in a multi-coloured patchwork coat with the usual accoutrement of rings and baubles and so on, is called to give evidence. It is then that Bill Smith sees the judge, who certainly clocked Bill and Polly Smith as soon as they came into the court room, give a slight nod of the head towards the two young lawyers.

So then Bill Smith's brain gets to work. You remember those tendrils in a Jackson Pollock painting, how they are a good representation of Bill Smith's thoughts, crossing over and intertwining until they finally emerge into the air, furiously sparking? Well in this case, with quite a shock, Bill Smith is suddenly aware of that sense he had on the tram that the two lawyers were not operating alone.

A few minutes later the court breaks for lunch and Bill and Polly Smith head down towards Place Pey-Berland. As they walk, Bill Smith discloses his hunch that the judge and the two lawyers are in cahoots. Polly Smith considers for a second and then replies that she has a hunch as well. So what they do is merge discreetly with a group of tourists that has gathered outside the cathedral to listen to their guide. This allows them to keep a discreet eye on Rue du Maréchal Joffre, which is the street that leads down from the courthouse towards the École Nationale de la Magistrature.

And it turns out that Polly Smith is right again because a few minutes later the Fox and the Boy come into view walking quickly down Rue du Maréchal Joffre and Polly says, 'Watch this,' and Bill Smith says, 'Well I never,' as the pair of them turn into the door of the École Nationale de la Magistrature.

And what that means, Dear Reader, is that this pair of murderous villains are not young lawyers at all but are in fact young magistrates, i.e. young judges in training. In other words this unpleasant pair will, in the fullness of time, become some of the most powerful people in Bordeaux.

CHAPTER EIGHT

Bill and Polly Smith did try, in their own small way, to have a Jack London style adventure. Bill Smith was reminded of this when Polly Smith declared at dinner one night, 'We all have gaps in our lives.'

They had been talking about an old friend with whom they had recently renewed contact. For a brief moment this friend, Frederick April, a cousin of Ludovic April whom we mentioned earlier, had been notorious. His picture and story were on the front page of *Sud Ouest* after he got caught out in a storm while on a hiking trip in the Pyrenees and had to be rescued by a helicopter. After that, Frederick went off to Paris, where it was rumoured that for a while he 'got religion' in a rather strange sort of way and it is only now, five years later, that he has popped up again, running a surf shack at Capbreton. Of course he is too old for it, but he has swept his hair back into a ponytail and spends his days in a wetsuit and people seem to accept him.

Polly ran into him when she was down there a couple of months ago and they had a good old chin wag. He told her that this was his fifth season running the surf shack but Polly, showing early indications of becoming a good detective, wasn't so sure and so she slipped into a cafe further down and asked and they said he had only opened it up that season.

Of course, now we have questions. What's it all about? Where has he been? To which, of course, the answer is that it is none of our business. Which is a long way around saying that Bill and Polly Smith also have a small gap in their narrative chronology.

After Bill Smith left the commercial photo laboratory and Polly Smith left the circus, they moved from Bordeaux to Brittany. Bill Smith insisted he was in need of a 'life-changing adventure', to which Polly Smith replied that she had all the adventure she wanted when she worked in the circus. But Bill Smith had got it firmly into his mind that he needed to feel the cold slap of Atlantic air on the face. He even referred to it as a getting bit of the 'old brine'. What he wanted, of course, was to have a Jack London style adventure before it was too late.

So Bill Smith got a job as a deckhand on a trawler out of a small Breton fishing port and Polly Smith got a job waitressing at a local cafe. The problem, which soon became apparent, was that Bill Smith is not one of the Jack London warrior caste. With that hangdog look and that old Bill Smith shuffle and the uncombed hair and the emerging pot belly, he is really a mild-mannered sedentary, one of the crowd: a spear carrier or bit part player. Knowing this, Polly Smith wondered how he was going to work out as a deckhand on a rough old trawler beating out of a rough old Breton seaport and being thrown around by Atlantic gales and having to put up with the rough old humour of the rough old crew.

Of course, Bill Smith didn't last past the first voyage on the trawler. On return to port, the skipper took him to one side and said, in that kindly way that sometimes rough old people can adopt, that perhaps he would be better suited to work ashore. The incident taught Bill Smith that frequently one half of the brain does not talk to the other half. He had known right from the beginning that he would not last five minutes on that trawler, but still he had gone ahead.

So Bill Smith got a job in a photographic shop on the quayside, selling postcards, ice cream and so on, to which he is much better suited. Eventually they returned to Bordeaux. Bill Smith had a chuckle and said, 'Well I learned a lesson about myself there.' But no one likes to admit to a failure so they shuffle around their narrative chronology to cover up that bit of their lives.

Bill and Polly Smith later noted, in the Musée d'Aquitaine exhibition, the Jack London quotation about being a 'superb meteor' in 'magnificent glow' and all that. Bill Smith reflected then that he had learned the hard way, from his experience aboard the Breton trawler, he was not the 'superb meteor' type.

It is after their return from Brittany that they set up as quayside photographers with their African grey parrot and then the Napoleon and Josephine costumes. Which, in a roundabout way, brings Bill Smith back to Jack London and the exhibition at the Musée d'Aquitaine.

Does anyone realise how short Jack London's life was? That he died in 1916 when he was just forty? Oh boy. He packed so much in. He started early and didn't waste a minute.

So Bill Smith is sitting at the kitchen table wondering if the *Snark* adventure could be a good 'hook' to interest a Hollywood producer in a new film on the life of Jack London.

He is developing this theme, citing in particular Jack following the trail of the cannibals that Herman Melville had encountered on Nuku Hiva in the Marquesas sixty-five years earlier, when Polly Smith calls out from the kitchen. There is a small domestic crisis. A lid has stuck tight on a jar and when that is done there is a carving knife that needs to be sharpened.

By the time he is finished in the kitchen half an hour has passed and Bill Smith has lost his place in the story.

Eventually he gets going again.

It is the autumn of 1906 and a chill wind is whipping across the Bay.

He stops, reads back the line and frowns. Then he straightens his fingers and adds another line.

In the springtime of 1906, San Francisco is struck by a terrible earthquake. For the record, the total is 3,000 dead and 80 per cent of the city destroyed. The quake strikes in April and turns the city on its head – and here comes the old cliche – so that it resembles a war zone: bridges gone, buildings tumbled down, etc., etc.

But of course – Bill Smith is typing quickly now – the press boys must have their green shoots. Editors need a daily miracle story which they can entitle, 'A Little Ray of Hope in a Desperate World'. So the gumshoe hacks and the photographers hurry down to the Anderson Ways shipyard where construction of the *Snark*, Jack London's 45-foot ketch in which he will adventure in the South Seas, is nearing completion.

Though he has the boyish good looks of a Jack Kennedy and that sense of adventure as already described, Jack London is an innocent abroad when it comes to money. As a result of financial miscalculations, debt collectors are chasing after Jack and his crew and are threatening to nail writs to the mast of the *Snark*. (But then if you have sent to Oregon for special timber for the boat construction it should be no surprise if you have gone over budget!)

When they finally leave San Francisco they don't even have the engine fitted. They've had to scoot away quick to avoid those debt collectors. The engine is strapped down in the hold and is eventually installed in Hawaii. And those boat builders, sensing a naive guy they can milk in the post-quake chaos, have also charged him a fortune and not done a good job at all. The *Snark* is seaworthy enough but she rolls like a pig and on the first leg to Hawaii her planks are letting in water so they have to bail constantly.

The crew is Jack, his wife Charmian and Charmian's 'kindly' uncle, Roscoe Eames, who will be their captain and navigator. It turns out that Roscoe Eames can navigate fine when he is in sight of land but is 'all at sea' when they are out in the ocean. Martin Johnson, who will later write his own account of the voyage, is the cook and there is another deckhand. And this is the kicker – or the rib-tickler as it used to be known: Jack London has hired a young Japanese lad as a cabin boy to serve them at table! So these amateur adventurers, setting off on their ill-prepared boat, will at least have that comfort. Such are the priorities of these adventurers. But don't kid yourself, Dear Reader; they are not a bunch of softies.

Bill Smith does a brief encapsulation.

During the *Snark*'s two-year, 10,000 mile voyage, Jack London and his crew confront terrible storms, suffer raging thirsts, meet savages with blackened and sharpened teeth and contract terrible leg ulcers. Across the South Pacific they take in Hawaii, the Marquesas, Tahiti, Samoa, Fiji, the New Hebrides, the Solomons and other coral reefs and rocky shores too numerous to mention. In other words, they have a real Jack London style adventure.

But a word of warning here.

Most of us, including Bill and Polly Smith, are better suited to being armchair adventurers. We can select our expeditions in library books and curl up in an armchair for an afternoon and lose ourselves. And when we come round from it all a couple of hours later we can think that was fun and no harm done and now we are all going to have a nice cup of tea.

So if you are already beginning to accumulate materials in your front room for a trip up the Amazon – canoes and paddles and supplies and so on – you had better be sure, before you set off, that you are of the Jack London 'warrior caste' and not the normal 'dreamy sedentary' type.

CHAPTER NINE

This is by way of an 'intermediate' chapter which you can skip, Dear Reader, if you are in a hurry. However, there is a sting at the end of the chapter which might be worth waiting around for!

So that evening, after supper, Bill and Polly Smith are out taking a stroll along the Quais. After the heat of the day it is always a pleasure to feel the cool breeze that comes off the river in the evening.

When they reach the new bridge, named after our former long-serving mayor, Jacques Chaban-Delmas (now sadly departed this life), Polly Smith stops and looks up at the clear night sky. She points out to Bill Smith a number of the constellations such as the Plough and Orion's Belt. Then she slips her arm around Bill Smith's waist and says all the things that people say when they look up at the constellations in the night sky, about the vastness and wonder of it all and so on.

But back in the apartment half an hour later, Bill Smith pours them both a glass of cognac and says, 'Those constellations you named – the Plough, Orion's Belt and so on – well do you know that if you looked at the night sky from another perspective you would see a different pattern?'

Half an hour later still, Polly Smith has gone to bed and Bill Smith is sitting in front of the old Underwood once again. After a few minutes, and with some hesitation, he starts to type.

Carl Jung and the editors of *Sud Ouest* make real strange bed fellows. But both are trying to fashion the world in their own particular way.

Bill Smith pauses briefly before continuing.

Carl Jung and the editors of *Sud Ouest* both have their own archetypes. And these archetypes are the 'scaffolding' on which our lives are based.

Bill Smith wonders if he is getting into water that is too deep. He taps the side of the typewriter with a pencil and frowns. The readers may think he is 'losing the plot'. He gets up and stretches his legs, then sits down again and decides to carry on typing.

Carl Jung has his mother figures and his father figures and his devil figures and his gods and all that, while the editors of *Sud Ouest* have their court cases and car crashes and political scandals and mayoral races and sporting events. But both sets of archetypes serve the same purpose. They put you on your feet for the day, set your compass right, give you a reason for getting up in the morning, if you like. But with *Sud Ouest* you have to make the distinction between the main paper, with all its regular items, and the mysterious back page.

Bill Smith gives a chuckle, remembering. He feels on firmer ground now. He is into the swing of the argument.

A couple of years ago Bill and Polly Smith had done a little test. They had turned off television, radio, internet, etc. They had also stopped reading the regular main section of the newspaper. Instead, they had taken their world view entirely from the mysterious back page of *Sud Ouest*. And, oh my Lord, how much better they were for it!

Their world view brightened and both Bill and Polly Smith said that at the end of the experiment they were treading with a light step and that they were also sleeping and eating well. If they had been circus animals you would have said their coats glistened. In fact, the back page of *Sud Ouest* gave Bill and Polly Smith so many talking points it quite filled up their day 'til they wondered where all the hours had gone.

Bill Smith is aware that there are times when this story veers off at an angle, or to rephrase that, at an improbable angle. There are perhaps parallels with circus performers in the Otto Dix etchings that we mentioned earlier. But in the case of the mysterious back page all we can suggest, Dear Reader, is that if you ever find yourself in Bordeaux do buy a copy of *Sud Ouest* and check out the back page and make up your own mind about it.

So the centrepiece of the back page is a large weather map of the South West of France, all done in lovely delicate yellows and blues and greens. Bill and Polly Smith think it is an artwork in its own right. It's surrounded by a series of smaller weather maps offering other valuable meteorological information.

Bill and Polly Smith spend time studying these maps. In their opinion this is a correct world view. Is there anything more important, as part of an 'underpinning structure' or a 'scaffolding', than the weather? Especially, you could argue, in this era of climate change. But these maps aren't a pushover, a quick glance and on you go. The editor demands of his or her readers a certain meteorological knowledge. But if you can read a barometric chart and understand the importance of tidal coefficients you will get the benefit.

World temperature comparisons become a talking point for the pair. When Polly Smith notes that Stockholm is consistently warmer than Brussels during most of February, that becomes a meteorological puzzle for them to solve. Then Bill Smith notes that it is minus twenty in Montreal for three days in a row and he thinks of the poor downed flyer stuck up there in the north. Moscow is a degree colder still. And when they see that Saint Pierre and Miquelon, and Wallis and Futuna have a temperature difference of almost thirty degrees, that develops into a spirited discussion on the future of the former French overseas territories. Of course, everyone knows where Saint Pierre and Miquelon is, but how many people can point out Wallis and Futuna? (Here is a clue: Jack London visited Futuna with the *Snark!*)

Once they have done the weather maps there are all the other panels to study. Take a date at random, say 8 February. Who knew that 8 February is the date of the first execution by gas in the USA, the date a new tomb in the Valley of the Kings in Egypt is discovered and that it is also the date of the birth of the Dada artistic movement? There is quite a bit for Bill and Polly Smith to discuss there!

When they want to go further afield and have some 'exotic', Bill and Polly Smith's imaginations are fired by stories such as the tale of the shopkeeper in Sumatra who came into work one morning to find an eighty-pound tiger trapped in his basement. Bill and Polly Smith speculate about how they would best deal with a situation like that. Polly Smith is for closing up the shop until the 'authorities' arrive to evacuate the tiger, while Bill Smith argues that providing the basement is secure there is no reason why the store should not remain open.

And then there is the story of the young man who tried to swim the fifteen miles from Moorea to Tahiti after missing the last ferry at night. That makes Bill and Polly Smith speculate on the over-confidence of youth today. Bill Smith adds that he is sure there had been drink taken. The young man survived, by the way.

And on it goes.

They read that, unusually, a Canard Mandarin has been spotted in Central Park in New York. A Canard Mandarin, it turns out, is a cutely coloured small duck normally at home in Northeast Asia. Bill and Polly Smith also discover that Buddhist monks in Thailand are developing an obesity problem because they are being offered hamburgers and chocolate cake, rather than the traditional rice and vegetables, by modern Thai housewives.

Bill and Polly Smith also get good on saint's days. They learn that Saint Margaret of Scotland (deceased 1093) introduced the Roman liturgy into that country and that Saint Gerald (deceased 1109) restored Christianity to Toledo following the defeat of the Moors.

And on the domestic front, well, here is something. How many people today know that bicarbonate of soda is an effective cure against bad breath? Or how about mimosa flowers; not many people know that, when dipped into a white of egg before being rolled into sugar to crystallise, they make excellent edible cake decorations?

But even in this ideal world things have to be paid for. So at the bottom of the back page is a picture and a 'come hither' advertisement for a large and expensive 4x4 jeep. This makes Bill Smith wonder if that is the jeep in which they could make their dream journey across the Sahara desert. So Bill Smith checks out the temperature for Dakar and sees that it is a very reasonable twenty-two to twenty-six. And so he thinks well, hold on, it could just be possible. And before they know it they've had an agreeable dinner with a good bottle of plonk and a long discussion about crossing the Sahara desert, which has involved getting atlases out and worrying about supplies you would take and whether you could carry enough water and so on.

It must be wonderful to be in charge of that back page operation, Bill Smith types, to thrum your fingers on the desk before sending out the office junior to check the time of moonrise that evening. Imagine that frisson of delight when you come across a story about a tiger in the basement of a shop in Sumatra or a Canard Mandarin being discovered in Central Park in New York (who you imagine, in an amused sort of way, may turn out to be a Chinese diplomat). And then you can't help thinking of Saint Gerald of Toledo and Saint Margaret of Scotland and wondering what it would have been like if those two could have met? And those jolly Thai monks … Bill Smith suspects that Saint Margaret of Scotland was neither jolly nor fat.

Both Bill and Polly Smith think that the editor of this page is very much in the style of Michel de Montaigne, i.e. a person of moderation, pleasant humours, both realist and reasonable and with an inquiring mind. They are interested in the time of moonrise and moonset and in comparative temperature charts of today and twenty years ago, as well as offering household tips and ways to get through one's daily life. In other words, they are offering their own set of archetypes that are about as good as Carl Jung's or anyone else's.

(By the way, and returning to Montaigne for a moment, did you know that his closest friend, Étienne de La Boétie, was carried away by the plague in 1563? That shook Montaigne. But in that era plague was always a threat. When it struck again in Bordeaux, in 1585, Montaigne 'confined' himself to his country estate outside the city. As to death itself, Montaigne said he would like to be taken suddenly when he was out 'planting his cabbages'.)

But if all of the above sounds too tame and if you are looking for some more 'bang', here comes that sting in the tail.

Bill and Polly Smith are sitting at breakfast when Polly Smith puts down her coffee cup and says, 'Well, how about that.'

The information she reads out to Bill Smith is contained in a panel called *'C'est le moment de ...'* which does not need any translation. So she reads, 'Statistics have recently been released which show that if a person goes missing the most likely place to find them, in any big city, is down by the station ...'

Bill Smith said later that had sent a shiver down his spine.

It also gave them their clue where to go next in the murder hunt.

CHAPTER TEN

The last time we mentioned Harold and Elizabeth and Dorothy Macmillan and Lord 'Bob' Boothby and all that business we left it on a cliffhanger, with talk of gangsters and even a serial killer, so it is time to deliver on that.

To recap: the PM, Harold Macmillan, has been cuckolded for more than thirty years by his former best friend Lord 'Bob' Boothby or, to give him his full moniker, Baron Boothby of Buchan and Rattray Head.

A 'guest appearance' by Philip has also been mooted.

Incidentally, in relation to that gentleman, Roger the Diplomat can attest that he lives up to his reputation of having what are called, in polite circles, 'sea-going manners.' Roger himself cites an instance when he and Elizabeth are taking tea on the terrace at Balmoral. Up strides Philip and addresses Elizabeth in his best sea-going manner. Then a minute later off he strides again, Roger ignored and Elizabeth left with a face like thunder.

But actually the richest character in the drama, by a country mile, is Bob Boothby.

Here is a 'pitch' that could tempt a certain type of American film producer. It is from a regular biography of Boothby with a dozen sentences jumbled up and placed in a new order.

'Bob Boothby, a regular recipient of the generous hospitality of Mrs Ronald Greville, Lady Astor, Lady Cunard, Lady Londonderry and Lady Colefax, is served lunch, which consists of langoustine mayonnaise, soufflé, a couple of bottles of champagne on ice and a bottle of Volnay topped up with brandy. Lunch over, Boothby writes to the Queen Mother to say that yesterday he played a round of golf with the Duke of York on the Home Course and that he (Boothby) will never forget his delight when he (the Duke of York) holed a long putt on the seventeenth green to beat him (Boothby) by 2 and 1. Later he goes for a flight over the grounds in Philip Sassoon's private airplane. When he goes up to change into black tie for dinner, he notes to his delight that there is a cocktail and carnation on his dressing table. Dinner is served that evening by six white-coated footmen and a large, fat butler whose name Boothby forgets. To round off the evening, Richard Tauber (who else) sings to them all under the stars.'

(A brief point of court etiquette here. The old rogue's correct title is actually Baron Boothby, though to his public he is always Lord Boothby. To his friends he is plain old Bob. And part of the appeal of his wonderful title is its sonority. You can alter the word sequence to change the emphasis. For instance how much more menacing is Baron Rattray of Boothby and Buchan Head!)

And then there are Bob's other 'peculiarities' which, if pitched correctly, might just 'hook' a film producer. You can tick them off on your fingers as you go.

That Bob is as clever as hell. He can read by the time he is four and is writing letters by the time he is six.

That Bob is a boozer. He can sink a bottle of Scotch in an evening, no problem.

That Bob is a gambler. Casino to stock exchange and all ports in between. You entrust money to him at your peril.

That Bob can have you in stitches. His cousin, Ludovic Kennedy, says he is the funniest man he ever met, though often coarse in the extreme.

That Bob is astonishingly progressive. In the 1920s he's arguing in parliament for a minimum wage and a form of universal income. The 1920s, for God's sake!

That Bob is both venomous and generous. He helps out many people, a lot of them undeserving. In his own phrase, if asked he would give his cat half a bottle of champagne.

That Bob, as well as being a ladies' man (Dorothy Macmillan et al.), also has an eye for the younger gentlemen – at the time strictly illegal.

That Bob frequently trawls low life clubs in the company of the Kray Twins and other infamous gangsters in search of these young gentlemen.

That Bob, when in disgrace after yet another 'upset', is frequently left in the flat at Eaton Square with only Gordon the Butler for company. Oh, what stories Gordon the Butler could tell if only he were with us now!

That Bob is at the centre of a scandal that rocks the country in the 1960s (details of which are coming up in a later chapter).

That Bob, in his later years, is one of the first of the radio and television commentator class and so becomes a household name.

That Bob is, overall, quite the buccaneer, though sadly by the end he gets so heavy that further swash and buckle is out of the question.

There is a last anecdote everyone tells about Bob Boothby. (If you are pitching it to a film producer it is important to get your timing right.) It's the 1930s. Boothby is in Germany and a meeting has been arranged with Hitler in Berlin. So Hitler comes into the room and everyone stands up and Hitler booms out, 'Heil Hitler!' at which Boothby jumps to his feet, faces off to Hitler and booms back, 'Heil Boothby!' Incidentally, in letters home directly after the meeting, Boothby correctly calls out Hitler as a 'wrong'un'.

So if the Hollywood producer is still interested then over a lunch (champagne and oysters on Sunset Boulevard) you can make your final 'pitch' to sell the old rogue thus:

Bob Boothby is a 22-carat gold English gentleman (Eton and Oxford) who has intelligence and courage by the bucket load. He never cares a fig for what anyone else thinks and is generous to a fault. So, overall, he has bloody style.

Bob Boothby is also a first-class example of the corrupt aristocracy which, with only a brief interregnum for Oliver Cromwell, has ruled over us all for so long.

And here you can add, with a final flourish, 'That corrupt aristocracy that has done so much to harm this green and pleasant land!'

Boom. Contract landed. Dollar bills all around. The Hollywood Mogul loves it. And why not? Isn't Boothby the character?

Bill Smith stops, reads back what he has written and knows that he has gone on far too long. He needs to wrap this up soon. So in conclusion and for the benefit of more regular readers he types: Bob Boothby is an excellent MP for Aberdeen and Kincardine. He is always fighting the good fight for the herring fishermen of those far-flung northern seas. But Bob Boothby can never be a candidate for serious government office: he is too erratic, irascible and independent. And certainly too clever. And certainly not trustworthy. It is as a loser's gift that he is given that splendid moniker Baron Buchan of Boothby and Rattray Head and elevated to the House of Lords. When he dies in 1986 (Dorothy having died twenty years earlier, in 1966) his ashes are scattered from the side of a Scottish trawler into the wide open ocean by his widow Wanda

– thirty years his junior and from Sardinia and by all accounts quite the little glamour puss.

And that is enough of Boothby for the moment.

Time to change the scene.

That night, over a glass of wine at the Café Français, Bill and Polly Smith are chewing over the events at the drugs trial. The revelation that the lawyers are, in fact, young magistrates and that they are in cahoots with the judge has been a real shock.

Bill Smith frowns and stops.

Actually he needs to get back to the story of those 'murderous magistrates' as quickly as possible. So here, briefly, is the final scene of this chapter. It further shows how the aristocracy bend the law to suit their needs.

Winter has given way to spring and so there is no fire in the study in Windsor, where Elizabeth and Roger are taking lunch. Elizabeth always calls Windsor a 'dreary old prison'. She is counting down the days until she can get away to Balmoral.

Roger is over from Japan for a good few months this time and has brought Haiku to England with him. They have been looking at universities; he is at that age. Elizabeth is insisting that the next time he visits her he brings Haiku along as well. One of the Japanese royal family has been over recently and Elizabeth is full of the visit. She says they swapped notes and she thinks by comparison she has it much easier here. On a professional basis, Roger is certainly interested in Elizabeth's insights into the Japanese monarchy.

But eventually Elizabeth returns to the Boothby affair, as Roger knew she would. She is still sensitive to the injustice done to her 'poor Harold.'

'Dorothy Cavendish was such a silly woman to get involved with Boothby,' she says. 'And why Harold ever married her in the first place I don't know.'

Roger puts down his knife and fork and looks at Elizabeth.

'I had heard,' he says – they are of the same generation and loosely related in a cousin-ish way, which means that he can get away with asking questions that others cannot – 'that it was actually Dorothy Macmillan who seduced Bob Boothby, not the other way round.'

'Oh, that old canard,' replies Elizabeth with a sharp laugh. Then she looks directly at Roger. 'Actually you're right. She was like the rest of the Cavendish family. A real hussy and quite shameless. Cavorting round like I don't know what. And she was such an ugly old thing. They say she had thighs like hams. I can't think for the life of me what Bob Boothby saw in her. Harold was totally humiliated.'

There is a pause for reflection. The tone of her voice softens for a moment.

'Of course, Harold was of my father's generation. You know that. He had such wonderful manners. Oh my goodness, how we used to laugh together.' She shuffles the remains of a trout meunière around on her plate before looking at Roger sharply. 'The affair had a dreadful effect on Harold's children: all of them disturbed. And the youngest, poor Sarah, never sure whether Harold was her father or whether it was the awful Mr Boothby.'

Elizabeth pushes the plate away and leans in towards Roger. Then she says in conspiratorial manner, 'Do you recall that doctor from Northern Ireland, the one with the strange name who practised in Eastbourne? Well last week the police finally let me see his file. They think he could have killed as many as 200 people!' She sits back and looks at Roger over the lunch table, eyebrows arched, as only Elizabeth can.

When the table has been cleared and coffee served, they are back to where they have been so many times before, chewing over the detail of that extraordinary trial. Elizabeth says 'the fix was put in' at a dinner in a hotel in Lewes during the committal hearing. Present at the dinner, according to Elizabeth, are the Lord Chief Justice, an ex-Attorney General and the chairman of the local magistrates. In recounting this tale (it is not the first time Roger has heard it from her) Elizabeth really does use phrases such as 'a can of worms was opened' and 'the fix was put in'. Those were Elizabeth's exact words, Roger says. In public, of course, she is impeccable. But in private she can be direct and demotic, he adds. Like Polly Smith, she enjoys her American detective stories.

Bill Smith stops typing and frowns. It is the same old problem; he is in danger, as ever, of getting the story down the wrong way round. Without some background it is going to be unintelligible. He will have to be as brief as possible but it is an excellent example of the perfidy of our governing class.

We are in the summer of 1950 and Edward Cavendish, the 10th Duke of Devonshire and head of the Cavendish clan, is on holiday in Eastbourne. Edward Cavendish is also, of course, Dorothy Macmillan's brother, which makes him Harold Macmillan's brother-in-law. Harold is, at that time, beginning a ministerial career that will take him right to the top as PM.

While on this holiday in Eastbourne, poor old Edward Cavendish has a heart attack and is attended by John Bodkin Adams, the Northern Irish doctor to whom Elizabeth has already referred. Dr Adams is practitioner to the wealthy in that town. And what happens next? Well, Edward Cavendish, aged fifty-five, very quickly keels over and dies. Which, as it turns out, is the fate of a lot of John Bodkin Adams' patients – usually after they have left him a little something in their will.

Police suspect Adams of doing this usually via a jab of morphine.

Eventually it all comes to a head – you cannot go on like that for ever – and in 1957 John Bodkin Adams is put on trial for the murder of two elderly Eastbourne ladies. And that date is important, because it's in 1957 that Harold finally lands the top job and becomes PM.

So the newspapers are all revved up. It's going to be the Trial of the Century. It's the talk of the pubs and clubs. Everyone is interested in the trial of a serial killer. But then Adams, against all the evidence, is acquitted on the main charges of murder although he is still struck off for falsifying death certificates. To put it mildly, there are a lot of questions to be answered as to the way the judge and the prosecution conducted the trial.

Incidentally, John Bodkin Adams is as strange a character as you could ever wish to meet. His family background is Plymouth Brethren in Northern Ireland. As to his personal life, he is strongly suspected of an all-male ménage à trois (then strictly illegal) with a local magistrate and a deputy chief constable! So for sheer bloody oddity John Bodkin Adams is certainly up there with the Cavendishes and the rest of them. But here is the question: what makes the establishment go all hugger-mugger and close ranks to protect someone so bloody odd and so totally undeserving as John Bodkin Adams?

Bill Smith's father, he of the cookhouse in the Canadian North, always used to say, when there was a problem that needed resolution, 'Well, chessboard it through, son.' While this was good advice, it was strange coming from a man who would first worry at a problem like a dog with a bone before finally deciding a course of action by the toss of a coin!

In the case of John Bodkin Adams, the logic of the chessboard leads directly to Harold Macmillan. The prosecution strongly suspects that the defence intends to bring in Edward Cavendish's death. This, the prosecution fears, may allow Dorothy's name to be dragged in, followed by Boothby's name and so the whole sordid affair will find itself in the public eye.

Elizabeth thinks that this would be a public humiliation that her 'dear Harold' might not be able to bear. So that is the reason why, as Elizabeth would say, 'the fix was put in', at that dinner in the hotel in Lewes.

So anyway here is a tip for a future serial killer, Bill Smith types. Target among your victims one of the most important aristocratic figures in the land, who also happens to be the brother-in-law of the PM, and you have got a good chance, if you are caught and brought to trial, of getting off.

In a later chapter we will disclose the extraordinary scandal that almost sank Bob Boothby, Bill Smith types. But for now that is enough of our wonderful British aristocracy.

CHAPTER ELEVEN

Bill and Polly Smith have made an elementary mistake in their hunt for the killers. As a result, their murder theory has been blown clean out of the water. So now there is a scene with the pair of them sitting at the breakfast table, both head in hand, both full of the glooms. Polly Smith is summarising the article in *Sud Ouest*.

'Three girls on a night out. (Two of the girlfriends of the drowned girl from Marseille have come forward.) Drink taken, blah-de-blah. They're larking about on the Pont de Pierre in the early hours, daring each other to walk along the parapet. Girl from Marseille stumbles, falls into the water. Total panic. Pitch dark. They run back to the Porte de Bourgogne side and scramble down the bank and plunge in themselves in a rescue attempt. Of course, the current is ferocious and they almost drown as well. Finally they wash back up on the bank, half dead. Then up comes the sun and home they go with still no one thinking to call the police. Apparently they are too traumatised and terrified. Only now, days later, have they finally plucked up courage to come forward. Etc., etc., etc.,' Polly concludes, putting down the paper with a snap.

'So that's the total collapse of our case,' Bill Smith says grimly.

The decision to hare off in the wrong direction, following a hunch rather than the evidence, has cost the rookie detectives precious time. But for the moment there is nothing further to be done. A new cruise boat full of gloomy passengers from Scandinavia has moored up at the Quais and they need to get to work.

It's not until the following day, with the cruise liner safely packed off to its next destination, that they're able to take up the chase again. In their minds has been that strange warning on the back page of *Sud Ouest*, which indicated that the best place to look for a missing person is down by the station.

So now it is just past six o'clock in the evening and Bill Smith is tucked away discreetly to the side of the Gare Saint Jean when he spots the two young magistrates stepping down from a tram.

'Well, well,' he mutters to himself.

The magistrates have undergone a change since the last time he saw them. There are dark lines under their eyes and their heads are down. They are like a couple of students who have ploughed their exams after too much partying and now they are hard up against the realities of the world.

Bill Smith thinks also that the old guilt may be raising its head. He smiles grimly to himself; if you do something like whack an old lady with the blunt edge of an axe or drown an innocent young bystander, that can set off a dose of the haunting. Bill Smith notes that, in a side pocket of his jacket, the Boy still has that dog-eared paperback.

When they have descended from the tram, the pair head over the tracks to the Café du Levant. Bill Smith, still angry about the time wasted following the false lead over the girl from Marseille, knows he has to take a chance if they are to crack the case. So he leaves the shelter of the station and crosses the tram tracks. He sits down at a table on the terrace outside the Café du Levant and orders a coffee from the waiter. He waits five minutes, enough to let everyone get settled, then takes a deep breath, gets up, pushes open the door and goes inside.

Unless you live in Bordeaux, Dear Reader, there is no reason you should know the Café du Levant. But to give you a brief heads up, outside it is all colourful tilework, which puts it somewhere between the Levant and the Orient, while the inside is in red flock, rather in the gaudy style of the Belle Époque. But the main thing, whatever your opinion of the décor, is that it is pleasantly cool after the great heat and the intense light of the outside. (Even at six or seven in the evening during the summer months it's still uncomfortable to be out. The sun, low in the sky, pins pedestrians, laser-like, to the pavement.)

The Café du Levant is what is known as a discreet 'meet-up' place so quite a few of the tables are already filled up with couples having a nice after-work drink. ('The couple were both married your honour, just not to each other.') The layout is that to the right there is a single row of tables while to the left there is more of an open space with tables dotted around. As Bill Smith makes his way to the back of the cafe he spots them by the far wall to his left.

The two young magistrates, the Fox and the Boy, are hugger-mugger and deep in conversation and – here you have guessed it, Dear Reader – they are of course with the judge who was presiding over the drugs trial at the Palais de Justice on the Place République. For a moment, as you can imagine, this leaves old Bill Smith quite wobbly in the leg department. The two magistrates are sitting with their backs to Bill Smith. So it is the judge, with his back to the wall facing in to the room, who clocks Bill Smith straightaway.

Bill Smith continues his progress. He's trying to remain calm. He's hoping his legs will carry him as far as the gents. Once there, he takes a deep breath and counts to thirty. Then he washes his hands, at the same time praying to God that one of the villainous crew doesn't barge in.

Bill Smith knows that the judge will be leaning forward to tell the Fox and the Boy that he has once again clocked Bill Smith. The judge has one of those elastic faces. If you were of a literary bent you would call it the face of a chameleon. His way of controlling his court, with a scowl and a good line in sarcasm, with the occasional joke and moment of indulgence thrown in, keeps everyone on edge. Right now he is certainly telling the young magistrates to hold their nerve, to show backbone and so on. When he is done lecturing he will turn more paternal. 'Don't worry,' he will say, 'the old judge will sort it out.'

Finally Bill Smith, loins girded, etc., etc., exits the gents and walks back through the cafe to the door. He glances casually to his right and, as you have guessed, the conversation of these three criminals (why call them anything else?) has stopped stone dead. The three of them are looking down, waiting for him to pass.

This gives Bill Smith a much needed shot of confidence. The three legal eagles are on the back foot. They don't know what Bill Smith's game is at all. And what judges and lawyers do not like is uncertainty; the only thing they hate more than uncertainty is coincidence. It messes up the whole legal structure.

And by the way, here is a tip. Never talk to a judge about Carl Jung and his theory of synchronicity. That gives them stone-cold nightmares. Because of course if Jung is right it blows the whole legal system out of the water. The bashing over the head or the heisting of the jewels may have nothing to do with regular cause and effect.

And of course there is that other terrifying moment when a defendant stands up and says, 'It was me unconscious what made me do it, guv.' That is the moment when the judge puts down his gavel and places his head in his hands and begins to weep. Because the whole legal system, which is based on a faux rationality, has been exposed as a house of cards. You might as well consult Madame Solaris in her cramped apartment in Quartier des Aubiers or ask the defendant what he had for his lunch and if it caused an indigestion which set off the frenzied knife-wielding attack. Without regular cause and effect the whole legal system collapses.

And at the end of one of these trials, if it is serious enough, the judge will probably have the brass neck to condemn someone to 'live' all alone in a concrete cell for the next ten or twenty years. As if anyone can deal with that; as if it were nothing very much, like a stay in a cheap hotel. The only way a judge should be allowed to do that is if he is prepared to do five years in solitary himself as part of his training.

So anyway, with that in mind, Bill Smith reaches the door and regains his table in the shade at the far side of the terrace and sits down to finish his coffee.

Just for a moment, can we go back to Jackson Pollock? He really is an important artist. If you look at his paintings you seem to have the whole pattern of your thought process mapped out in front of you. There is also a further complication. Because when those thoughts are making their way down the brain tendrils and crossing and inter-connecting they are actually going at different speeds!

Let me give you an example, Bill Smith types. A speeding car is hurtling towards you, so what you do is step out of the way pretty damn quick. For the moment you are concentrated on that. But here is the clever bit: the brain has still clocked the other stuff that is going on. It has seen the lady in the short skirt walking the one-eyed poodle who has also stepped out of the way to avoid getting splashed by the speeding car. But this information is being kept back for consideration later on. When the imminent danger of being run over is past, you can go back over the event and replay it. Then you can say to yourself well I never, I wonder how that dog lost its eye? It is your mind's eye that has seen and recorded it.

That's a lovely phrase, 'mind's eye'. If Bill Smith owned a racehorse he would certainly call it Mind's Eye. Or if he had a holiday house down by the beach – the type of place where, at least in England, they call them by names such as The Haven or Travellers' Rest or even Key Largo if you want to show off that you have visited Florida – well, if Bill Smith had a holiday hideaway like that, he would certainly call it Mind's Eye as well.

Two women come to sit at a table between Bill Smith and the door to the Café du Levant. Bill Smith looks over at the Gare Saint Jean, which is directly opposite him. It's a railway station in the classic nineteenth-century style. If you were to show someone who has never visited Bordeaux – say an American living in New York – a picture of the Gare Saint Jean, but with the name of the station removed then he (or she) would say without hesitation, 'Well that is certainly a railway station.' In front of the station trams rattle past in both directions, only stopping to disgorge weary office workers who hurry into the station to catch their train home.

So this square in front of the station is a real busy place. There are buses and trams and taxis buzzing round everywhere. There are a dozen colourful cafes and a few hotels. Because it is evening, the sun is low but the heat is still there. Flocks of starlings are singing their heads off in the plane trees that give shade for the cafes. Let us hope that our esteemed Mayor Alain Juppé, feeling liverish one morning, does not allow these ones to be cut down in the same way as he did in Place Gambetta.

So Bill Smith is sitting there turning everything over in his mind's eye. He is going over it frame by frame when suddenly he says – out loud in fact, so that the heads of the two women sitting next to him turn – 'Oh my goodness me, what a silly old Bill Smith I have been.'

Those Jackson Pollock-style tendrils containing his slow-moving thoughts, the ones playing catch-up, are finally beginning to spark and light up. It is like you see in the movies: that loose electrical wire sparking dangerously in the middle of a storm. Because sitting on the table by the judge is a box and everyone who lives in Bordeaux – everyone who lives in France – knows what that is. It is, of course, a cake box. Because that is what French people do. They buy a little cake and have it done up in a box with some nice ribbon and if they have been a naughty boy when they get home they give it to their angry wife in the hope that they will get forgiven or at least they will have their dinner put in front of them and not thrown at their head.

But here is the rub, as old Shakey-bakey used to say. The cake box is yellow and tied with red ribbon with the knot done in a particular, intricate way. There is only one patisserie in Bordeaux which uses yellow cake boxes tied up with that intricate red ribbon knot and that, of course, is Patisserie Solaris. And Patisserie Solaris is pretty much en-route from the Palais de Justice to the Gare Saint Jean.

So then all the tendrils are sparking and lighting and connections are being made all over the place. Then suddenly there is a great heave and a surge of electricity down said tendrils and Bill Smith realises, with a whoosh that partially lifts him from his chair, that of course it is Gloria, missing from work at Patisserie Solaris, who is their victim! So it is certainly she who is now lying at the bottom of the river weighted down and being nibbled by the fishes.

It takes Bill Smith a few minutes to regain his poise after this revelation. In fact, you could say he is quite shaken. But finally he gets up, crosses the road and the tram tracks and finds a spot by the entrance to the station, from where he can observe the door of the Café du Levant without being seen himself.

Finally the two young magistrates exit the cafe but they are without the judge. If they do not want to be seen together this is a further indication that they are up to no good. Bill Smith notices a difference in their step. They are heads up; their movement is more confident. The pep talk from the judge has straightened the backbone.

But of course the judge has his own interest to protect. He does not want these two boyos – who are only young boyos not long weaned off their mother's milk and still wet behind the ears – to get that guilty feeling about doing in poor Gloria and in a fit of remorse go beetling off to the law, or start blabbing in a bar or, God help us all, confess to some nosey priest.

But events take a turn that surprises Bill Smith when the two magistrates, instead of crossing the tram tracks to the station, continue along past the Hôtel Le Quebec and then turn up a street to the right. Bill Smith knows that this is a new element in the story. It could mean that the two magistrates have a discreet pied-à-terre somewhere in the vicinity of the station.

While Bill Smith is still pondering over this, the door to the Café du Levant opens again and the judge steps out, attaché case in one hand and cake box in the other. He crosses the road towards the station. Now that he is not behind his bench, Bill Smith can see that the judge is broad and stocky, a physique which matches the earlier noted rolled-over shoulders that many rugby players have.

Incidentally Polly, after their morning in the courthouse, starts to call him the Bristler, which Bill Smith reckons, as he watches him approach the station, is spot on. And a very unpleasant Bristler at that, he thinks. Bill Smith shivers when he thinks of poor Gloria's fate.

The judge crosses the tram tracks. It is only now that Bill Smith realises there is quite a 'social distance' between the judge and his two protégés. The young magistrates are class, anyone can see that; they have that peculiar effortlessness. Have we already used the word 'entitlement'? Another good description is 'top drawer', as in the phrase 'they are out of the top drawer'. By contrast, the judge is a very different character; his gait and posture and lived-in face tell the world that he has clawed his way up from the bottom.

The judge enters the station and passes just a few feet from Bill Smith before giving a quick check up at the departure board followed by a rapid glance at his watch. Which tells Bill Smith that the judge is a regular and that this is his normal homebound commute. Any seasoned detective operating a 'tail' would draw that conclusion. Bill Smith watches the judge dip into a kiosk, to emerge a few minutes later with *Sud Ouest*. No guesses as to what information he is checking for there!

And now, Dear Reader, you can read this passage about how Bill Smith followed the judge on the train. It will cast light on the character of the judge, and might give you a chuckle, but in terms of 'moving the story on' it is not up there with the events that have already been recorded. In other words, if you are in a hurry and your supper is waiting you can skip it. Up to you.

On the platform the judge turns to the right, so Bill Smith counts to five and follows him. He wishes he had an American private eye style trilby hat to tip forward but the judge doesn't turn around. He's not thinking that Bill Smith is following him. Also, he's not heading for one of the mainline trains that will take him inland. Instead, with attaché case in one hand and cake box in the other, he boards a little two-car boyo that will end up by the sea at Arcachon.

And it is here that Bill Smith has a stroke of luck because, as he boards the train himself, he sees the tail end of the judge (he must have dallied a little), disappearing up to the top carriage, i.e. the train is a double decker. The railways here in France are modern and up to date, not like the old grinders they still have in Britain. But even in this modern, egalitarian world the upstairs is marked as 'First Class'. And who more deserving of first-class travel than a judge? Bill Smith checks out the carriage, sees that there are stairs front and back up to the top deck and chooses a seat where he can discreetly cover both.

So that is how they travel down towards the sea that evening. The conductor passes and Bill Smith buys a ticket. Then he looks out of the window and notes that thunder clouds are beginning to build from the south. He thinks about the judge. He will be leafing through *Sud Ouest* but will find nothing. Bill Smith knows this, having already read *Sud Ouest* that morning. The judge puts the paper down to gaze out of the window. His glance occasionally drops to the cake box at his side.

In the carriage below, private eye Bill Smith keeps his lonely vigil.

The train slows and stops at country stations and people get on and get off but there is no move from up top. If he is going right through to the end, to Arcachon, that will suit Bill Smith. It is always easier to follow a suspect in a crowd. Without a trilby hat to tip over his eyes it would be difficult to follow the judge out of a one-horse country station.

So here we go, Bill Smith types. Our train is finally drawing into Arcachon. Everyone knows Arcachon and the seaside. It's kind of anonymous and androgynous. It's full of little old richies with silver hair and perfect teeth. In the summer they are joined by their beautiful families and their tousle-haired grandchildren. So the judge comes down the stairs and exits the train and Bill Smith, already slipping easily into his role as private eye, discreetly follows.

And here, Dear Reader, is what happened next. Actually it's quite a gas, if you're still with us.

The judge is standing there outside the station, phone to his ear, and he is frowning. There is also that slight scrunching back of the lips which, in a courtroom context, certainly means trouble ahead. What he has been anticipating, Bill Smith surmises as he loiters discreetly in the station doorway, is that his wife is going to pick him up in the car. But it looks as if this is not going to happen. Bill Smith puts two and two together and thinks that this is the problem to which the cake from Patisserie Solaris is the answer.

So the judge is looking around and there are other people hailing taxis and getting into cars driven by faithful spouses. And, this being a modern world, there is even an elegantly dressed business woman being picked up by a house-husband with an infant toddler strapped into a car seat in the back. A few anxious pedestrians look up at the sky, which is beginning to darken. They can feel the wind starting to get up. But then they toss a mental coin and, betting they can beat the coming downpour, set off at a brisk pace on foot.

Bill and Polly Smith come down here to the sea to get out of the city during the summer heat. Bordeaux is what is called a 'mineral city', which means there is not a lot of green. In summer it can turn into an oven. That is why Mayor Juppé's decision to allow those trees to be cut down and much of Place Gambetta to be concreted over was so stupid.

Bill and Polly Smith love the sea salt smell and the scent of pine trees when they step off the train here. But this is not a town where they could ply their trade. You could not dress up here as a clown and expect to get a sympathetic reaction. You need a lot of money to live in a town like this.

The judge returns phone to pocket with a snap. He is sniffing the air and looking up at the sky, the same as Bill Smith is doing.

He decides against walking. Instead, he goes up to the taxi rank, speaks to a driver and gets into his cab. Bill Smith counts to five and, just as the judge's taxi moves off, advances forward quickly and – in the best tradition of private eyes in the movies – says to the next cabbie in the rank, 'Follow that cab.' He takes a note out of his wallet as they go up the hill towards the Ville d'Hiver.

Now the Ville d'Hiver is a very odd place indeed. Do you have the patience for a quick diversion?

Well, 100 or so years ago Arcachon was a small fishing village. Then the railway was put in from Bordeaux and suddenly Arcachon was fashionable both for vacations and as a health resort. Then the brothers Emile and Isaac Pereire, the hotshot businessmen of their time, built a series of gigantic mansions in the Ville d'Hiver in the oddest gothic style, all turrets and towers and so on. So what you ended up with was a whole series of residences that look like minor Rhineland castles. These in turn attracted aristocracy and royalty from all over Europe.

But here is the really odd bit. Over the years trees have grown up around the mock castles and because they are built on hills and slopes they have become part of the landscape. They have views down to the Bassin d'Arcachon. So now they are quite charming, in a mad Hollywood sort of way. Of course, the dukes and princes are long gone and most of the mansions are divided into apartments but some are still in the hands of the little old richies.

So here we are, entering the Ville d'Hiver, when the judge's taxi pulls up and Bill Smith barks, 'Stop!' at the same time. He gives the cabbie the note he has in his hand and says, again in the style of the movies, 'Hey, keep the change, buddy.' Then he slips out of the taxi and ducks into a driveway. He can see the judge fifty yards ahead.

So now the sky has darkened and the wind is up and the storm is approaching. The judge walks down to his house and

Bill Smith can tell straightaway that he is in trouble because the BMW that should be in the driveway is not there. What has happened is that the long-suffering wife – no, change that to blonde-haired trophy wife, Bill Smith types – has departed with the fitness instructor.

Dotted between the mock castles are more modest houses. Bill Smith thinks that Americans would call them ranch houses. By comparison with the gothic mansions in between which they are sandwiched they are modest affairs. It is to one of these houses that the judge is briskly walking. So of course the pieces are beginning to fall into place now and we can see that the judge is a real social climber. He can tell work colleagues in Bordeaux, 'Hey, ya know I live in the Ville d'Hiver at Arcachon,' and his colleagues think he is old money and living in a mansion and so on.

So anyway, the wind is up now and the sky is dark as hell, indicating that the rain is imminent, and the judge, discreetly observed by private eye Bill Smith, is juggling attaché case and cake box as he reaches into his pocket, fumbling for keys. Finally he puts the key into the lock, all with a huffety-puff-puff, i.e. a show of bad temper and impatience. And of course what happens – you have guessed it, Dear Reader, especially if Bill Smith's guess with the trophy wife is correct – is that the key doesn't fit the lock. So he takes a step back and looks up at the shuttered windows and there you go. Even for the judge, the message has finally got down the brain tendrils and the electricity is surging through. And so Bill Smith and the judge both say in unison, 'The bitch has changed the locks.'

But the surge of electricity down the brain tendrils has not finished yet. There is another burst coming down now. Try this on for size, because it occurs to the judge and Bill Smith at the same time: what if the trophy wife has discovered what the judge is up to? She could have picked up a message left on the voicemail. Trophy wives are generally pretty smart. Then if she has gone rooting through this and that she could have found that M stands for murder. Then you could say also that B stands for Blackmail. And then there is the letter R, which of course stands for the word Ruinous – as in extremely expensive divorce settlement.

So what happens next is that, having checked windows and doors front and back, the judge pauses and looks with kind of a surprised stare at the cake box, which he still has in his hand. It is quite comic as Bill Smith relates it to Polly Smith later. Then it's the way he lifts the lid of the rubbish container and drops in the cake box. He does it with a horrible scowl on his face.

And then he is passing by Bill Smith, going at speed on foot, head down, bristling and livid, as the first clap of thunder sounds and the first drops of rain fall.

And soon our old judge, Bill Smith writes, mastermind of murder most foul of poor and harmless Gloria, will be in a bar in Arcachon with a large gin and tonic, ringing round other girlfriends to see who will give him a bed for the night. It will be the following day, when he is in his cups, Bill Smith writes, that he will realise that when the trophy wife has finished with him he will be lucky if he has a pot to piss in.

CHAPTER TWELVE

'I know what happened,' Bill Smith tells Polly Smith when he gets home.

She takes his soaking wet coat and hangs it up in the bathroom.

'You should have taken an umbrella.' She looks at him warily. 'Everyone knew a thunderstorm was forecast. You'll be lucky not to catch pneumonia.'

After that she sits Bill Smith down in a chair and begins to vigorously dry his head with a towel. All the time Bill Smith is trying to tell her what he has found out but his voice is muffled by the towel, so it isn't until he has been dressed in new clothes and is sitting down at the kitchen table with a cup of hot chocolate in front of him that he is able to tell Polly Smith that the two magistrates and the judge met up in the Café du Levant and that later he followed the judge to Arcachon.

Then he recounts the story of the judge being locked out of his house and his theory that a trophy wife is involved and that makes Polly Smith laugh. But when he tells her that because of the colour of the cake box the judge is carrying and by the intricate way the string is tied he is sure it came from Patisserie Solaris she begins to look serious. When he adds, finally, that Madame Chopsticks told him that Gloria had not arrived at work the other day, Polly Smith's head drops and she says, 'Oh my God.'

When Polly Smith recovers her composure, Bill Smith types, they go over the evidence again. They conclude that Gloria is certainly the victim but, as there have been no further reports in *Sud Ouest* of dead bodies being found in the river, there is still a chance, if only a slim one, Bill Smith says grimly, that they might find her alive.

That evening they hold a council of war over a glass of wine at the Café Français. Bill Smith tells Polly Smith that she will have to take over the shadowing duties as he has been compromised.

'The villains know my face and will be on the lookout for me,' he says.

Then Bill Smith sees that Polly Smith has a question to ask but she is unsure how to formulate it. So he says, 'Penny for 'em,' and Polly Smith says, finally, that the puzzle is the motive.

'Gloria is from El Salvador,' she says, 'so are we talking a drugs connection here, Bill? Could the judge and the magistrates be involved in a drug-smuggling plot? And have we got a double-cross going on?'

Bill Smith replies that, while a drugs connection cannot be ruled out, he has his own particular theory. He says that if he is right it is grim and unpleasant but not without a certain warped logic. Then he adds, in a firm manner, that he does not want to say anything more at present.

So that night Bill and Polly Smith go to bed with their minds all in a muddle. In their sleep they turn restlessly. It is as though their brains are in a big old mental washing machine. The livid face of the judge looms up in their dreams. He is buying a cake from poor Gloria in Patisserie Solaris. Then he is shouting at her and hauling her away, tied up with a rope.

To make it more confusing they have drifted off to sleep with that radio station in Northern Quebec, the one that is giving them their news of the hunt for the Norwegian Flyer, still playing. So that means that, in their dreams, local weather and traffic reports for Northern Quebec get mixed up with horrible images of poor Gloria being hurled off the Pont de Pierre by the two villainous magistrates.

But then sometime during the night a part of their brains registers an excited newsflash from the local radio station; the plane with the downed flyer has been sighted and a couple of tough old parachutists in survival gear are being dropped in. Bill Smith turns over. In his dream he is about to parachute into Patisserie Solaris himself. He is going to rescue poor Gloria. But then Polly Smith bursts in at the crucial moment. She is shouting that he cannot be a parachutist because he is too old and his knees are too stiff.

But to advance and explain the story by a couple of scenes …

The search HQ has asked the pilots of the jetliners that traverse the Atlantic to keep a lookout as they cross the search area. And now one of them, looking down, has spotted a thick plume of black smoke. So he calls out to his co-pilot, 'I reckon that's the flyer who went down and he is burning a tyre from his plane to alert us.' And so they radio in the position to the search HQ and suddenly everyone, especially the English Rose, is on a high old roll of excitement. But of course she has never given up because she is powered by love, which is the most potent rocket fuel of all.

So then a search plane with a couple of those tough old parachutists aboard is scrambled and then all anyone can do is wait and pray and hope that it is not a false alert. The smoke plume is way to the west of the regular search box, so it seems the young Norwegian Flyer was lured by the dipping sun as recounted earlier. It turns out that Madame Solaris was spot on as well.

This makes Bill Smith wonder. In their efforts to crack the case of the disappearance and possible murder of Gloria, they have learned by bitter experience that you need a solid foundation of fact to build a case. In other words regular cause and effect. And yet Carl Jung and Madame Solaris – and you could say Jackson Pollock – get there by intuition. So how is that? That is a puzzle that Bill Smith is, at the moment, unable to solve.

With Jackson Pollock there is a little clue. Go and search around, Bill Smith types, until you find that film of him doing one of his paintings. Bill Smith has watched it several times. He even got Polly Smith to watch it with him. The canvas is on the floor. Everyone knows that Jackson Pollock painted on the floor. But it is the way he is putting on the paint that is the clue. He is not doing it in a normal painterly manner. You know, standing by an easel saying 'ah' and 'um' and deciding to put a fine line there or a calculated dash here. Jackson Pollock has a gentle swaying rhythm. He is almost ladling the paint on. Polly Smith describes it as a farmer throwing out his seed corn. It is a regular motion. Almost hypnotic, Bill Smith adds. Ritualistic, like a priest with a censer, swinging and swaying as he walks up the aisle. Or perhaps like a slow dance. Or the rhythm of the wind or the sea, Polly Smith adds. And when you look at it later what the clever guy has done is to copy exactly that fractal system of nature, where patterns are replicated so precisely. So it looks like his brain has short-circuited the normal processes.

But there are other, more regular, questions that also need answers, Bill Smith types. For instance, why did the Norwegian Flyer wait so long to rip a tyre off the plane and douse it in petrol and set it alight and send up a thick plume of black smoke for rescuers to see? The answer, of course, is that no one knows how they will behave in a crisis until the crisis arrives. Look at the friends of the girl from Marseille. They panicked and waited days before they called the police.

In their attitude to those jetliners that whizz people so quickly between the continents Bill and Polly Smith are in opposite corners. Bill Smith thinks the jetliners are a regular marvel and are not appreciated by many of the people who ride in them. Take, as an example, the passengers who are alerted by the pilot on a traverse of the Atlantic to look out of the window because they are flying over the snow-capped mountains of Greenland. There is an argument to say that those who do not look down and get a thrill out of that (always remembering that you are in the fuselage of a rocket with a skin no thicker than half your thumb and that you are seven miles up in the sky), should not be counted as sentient beings and should be put in the slug or lettuce department.

Polly Smith takes the opposite view. She says she would never go in a jet-fuelled rocket where, if the slightest thing goes wrong – a grain of sand in a fuel pipe for instance – then that is curtains for you. She says that is why people keep the blinds down and play video games. She adds that Bill Smith is cruel to say it is because they are non-sentient beings who should be compared to slugs or lettuce. Polly Smith argues that jetliners should be banned because they are pushing out so much filth from their rear ends that they will make the planet uninhabitable in a few years' time.

As has been said before, if this tale should survive for any length of time either in paper form or in electronic form – and by the way do you know that a copy of every book published has to go to the British Library in London so hopefully that building will survive – well then Bill and Polly Smith would like to say a great big 'mea culpa' to future generations reading this account for all we have done to wreck our lovely planet.

Bill Smith stops typing for a moment and shakes his head sadly before continuing.

The Great Plague from which we are suffering at the time of writing is only old Nature's opening shot. Stuff that is coming down the track with climate change, etc., is ten times worse. You have been warned.

And to continue with that theme for a moment, there is actually a perfectly good way to cross the Atlantic if you must do so, rather than staying at home to observe everything locally. (Although, incidentally, if you do decide to stay home you will find there is so much to see there if only you open your eyes.) So in the old days the normal way to cross the Atlantic was by boat. Of course you think, because you are a hard-working something or other, that you cannot afford the time. Well of course now it is only a moment's research to discover that you can take your office with you!

You can certainly do all your busy-busy stuff from a computer in your cabin. They all have excellent communications systems these days. This is another modern world wonder. And when you have finished you can go up on deck and take in the sea air and talk with the crew and watch the gulls wheeling and the sea changing and if you are far enough north you will be able to see some of those giant bergs (if they have not all melted) in the distance. And you will probably have a bit of a blow and the ship will go up and down and you can go 'woo hoo' and 'waa haa' and when you finally dock in the New World you will have dozens of exciting stories to tell.

And funnily enough it does not cost that much because I am not talking about those swanky cruise ships that come up the River Garonne and into Bordeaux but one of those cargo boats that take a few passengers. It is not quite a Jack London adventure, but if a big storm blows up when you are making your crossing it will certainly get you into that area.

Anyhow, this is a long way round of saying that the game is on again for the stranded Norwegian Flyer and the injured Inuit lady.

So now, the night passed, Bill and Polly Smith have woken from their disturbed sleep. They have got up, washed their faces, brushed their teeth and in the case of Bill Smith – sad to say and not to be repeated – put in a plate with a couple of false teeth. Working as a quayside photographer does not allow for fancy implants. Finally they are sitting at the breakfast table across from each other, both of them dead silent, trying to get to grips with the news that penetrated their sleep in the early hours.

Eventually Bill Smith opens his mouth to speak and Polly Smith says she does not want to talk about it, especially at breakfast. So Bill Smith says, 'Well hold on; what would you have done?' and, 'Think of Herman Melville and what he saw in the Marquesas and also what Michel de Montaigne had to say on the subject.'

But none of this is a reassurance to Polly Smith, who reverts to a childhood stance – she does this literally and it is a strange sight, especially at the breakfast table and also considering she is a grown woman and not an emotional teenager – but she really does put her fingers in her ears to stop Bill Smith repeating the first words the pilot says to the two parachutists which are, 'Welcome to the camp of the cannibal.'

And I'm afraid there are more details to come. So, Dear Reader, if you are of a nervous disposition you might consider skipping a few paragraphs because, well, it all gets a bit grisly.

Polly Smith is still not reassured when, later in the morning, Bill Smith quotes what Michel de Montaigne had to say about cannibalism.

By way of explanation, Montaigne's time is the sixteenth century which, like ours, is an age of discovery. The Americas have been found, which is like going to the Moon or to Mars today. So when a group called the Tupinambá, from what is now Brazil, come on a visit to France, Montaigne goes up to Paris to meet them. He has heard that they practise cannibalism. He finds it's not done willy-nilly. They don't clamp their gnashers into any old dead body; it's all done with regulation and respect and ritual and so on. Montaigne also makes comparison with what is done to people when they are still alive. He instances the moment when the citizens of Bordeaux rebelled against a salt tax imposed by the government in Paris. The revenge taken by the government in Paris is so brutal and crude that you do not want to know the detail. After that, Montaigne writes, 'Which is better: to eat a man when he is dead or to torture him to death when he is still alive?' You might also compare with our modern times, when people are sentenced to live for ten or twenty years in a small concrete cell by one of those cruel judges.

And then again, Bill Smith says, look at what Herman Melville finds when he visits Nuku Hiva in the Marquesas. He describes the valley of Taipivai as a little garden of Eden, full of plenty, where on occasion cannibalism (strictly controlled) is practised. And then, Bill Smith adds, you can make the comparison with what Jack London found when he visited the same valley sixty-five years later. This is after the arrival of the Europeans and all the diseases they brought. The houses are in ruins and the people who have not left are all sick and living in poverty.

Though, Bill Smith types, that's not to say that cannibalism is necessarily a good thing; there is always the caveat that you do have to be careful from a health point of view. As everyone knows, our esteemed former president, Jacques Chirac, contracted the dementia after one too many meals of calves' brains.

None of which convinced Polly Smith. Not one jot at all.

So anyway, to finish up with here is the grisly detail of what the parachutists discovered – if you can stomach it.

When they hear that opening phrase, 'Welcome to the camp of the cannibal,' the two parachutists think it is just the ravings of a man driven out of his mind by the conditions he has had to endure. But then – and this is how they recount it, one of the parachutists spots an axe inside the makeshift tent up against what looks like the partly butchered hump of an animal. And of course, when they investigate, it is not an animal at all but it is, as you have guessed, the remains of the Inuit lady who fought the polar bear using what is called hysterical strength.

When they pull the cover back, what they find is that one of her legs is missing. The Norwegian Flyer explains to the tough old parachutists that she was killed when the plane crashed and did not suffer at all. He then shows them the bag where he keeps the flesh he has cut off. He explains that he thaws the meat out by warming it up in his sleeping bag during the night.

Later on, the medical guys down in Quebec City, who are trying to figure out what has been going on, get their break when they discover that the English Rose weighed the Inuit lady only a few weeks before, as part of a medical campaign. So, using as their principal tool of investigation a set of weighing scales, the medical investigators do a simple but still cool-headed piece of deduction. They weigh the body again and compare it to the previous weighing, which allows them to figure out how much flesh the Norwegian Flyer has hacked off.

And then – and this is the clever bit – they take the Norwegian Flyer's bag in which he has stored the meat he has cut off the leg with the axe. Then they weigh that as well and do the calculation to work out how much meat the Norwegian

Flyer has actually consumed. And, well, it turns out to be quite a lot – which is maybe why, when he is given a medical examination, he is found to be in surprisingly good condition and to even have gained a little weight. It may also explain why he greeted the two parachutists with a smile and a burp and with a toothpick in the side of his mouth. And it may also explain why, as an act of sensitivity, his first words were edited. Because what he actually said was, 'Welcome to the camp of the cannibal. Would you care for a little light lunch?'

Bill Smith stops typing. He sits back and smiles. Not bad, he says to himself. Not bad at all.

The next scene takes place that evening. Our pair of intrepid sleuths have made their way once more down to the Gare Saint Jean. They have gone on foot in case the magistrates are on board the tram and they are clocked. At the station they stand in the same discreet spot to the side of the main entrance where Bill Smith had stood before. There, they can monitor passengers descending from the tram but remain incognito themselves.

Incidentally, Dear Reader, if you ever find yourself in Bordeaux, then as well as all the regular sites that will be pressed on you by the eager beavers who work in the tourist office there is a sight that you should not miss, which is the pre-war railway map of the South West of France in the Gare Saint Jean. It's done in the form of a mural. It's recently been retouched and brushed up in the manner of an art work. When you enter the station it's on the far wall to your left. It is enormous, you can't miss it. You could certainly call it, in the English sense of the word, 'grand'. The people in those days stood firmly on their feet and knew their place – and the place of France – in the world.

Anyhow, the plan works like a dream because, just after six o'clock, who descends from the tram but our two young magistrates – without of course the judge. Bill Smith leans over to Polly and points them out. They have decided that it is Polly who will do the tailing, because of course by now Bill Smith is well known to the magistrates.

This evening the two young killers do not head over the road to the Café du Levant, as before, but they head up past the Hôtel Le Quebec and the Hôtel Regina before turning right up the Rue Pierre Loti. Polly Smith trails a discreet fifty yards behind, a baseball hat pulled down over her eyes because, Dear Reader, do you remember that the two magistrates did in fact glimpse her at that Jack London exhibition in the Musée d'Aquitaine? However, that was only fleeting and she was in a long floral skirt and so on, which is what she likes to wear normally. So today she is dressed in plain track suit, with hair tucked up under the baseball cap and with dark glasses. When she is home later that night and they are chewing it over she tells Bill Smith that she is 100 per cent sure she was not clocked.

But this is interesting: even though the two young magistrates – the Fox and the Boy – do not clock Polly, they still take a circuitous route home, showing that they are on the alert. A couple of times the Fox stops at a corner to peer into a shop window and Polly Smith has to slow and tip her head forward to stay hidden. Bill Smith types that this is a classic tactic on the part of the Fox because what he is doing is using the glass as a mirror to see if there is anyone coming up behind them.

So in this zigzag and roundabout sort of way, which is taking them in an easterly direction towards Nansouty, they approach L'Église de Sacré Coeur, which everyone knows is an awful old barracks of a church. It is then that Polly Smith turns the corner of a street and is forced to take a pretty smart step back because what she has seen is the two magistrates stopping at a house on the left-hand side further up the street.

The Fox looks back down the street but luckily Polly Smith has ducked back in time. She counts to ten before peeking out again. She is just in time to see the backs of the magistrates going into the house. She clocks that the house is near the end of the street and the door is a faded yellow.

Five minutes later, leaving time for the magistrates to get settled, Polly Smith walks as normally as she can, though her heart is thumping fit to burst, past the house with the yellow front door. With a sense of relief she turns into a narrow lane to the left and is soon in the shadow of the church. She counts back from the end of the row of houses until she is standing at the back of the magistrates' house.

Polly steps up to the back garden wall and, on tiptoe, peers over. It's a single-storey row house, what is called an 'échoppe' house in Bordeaux. Polly can see an untidy garden, a back door, a window. No lights showing. A couple of minutes later, a plan formulating in her mind, she is walking briskly back down to the Gare Saint Jean to meet Bill Smith, who has been patiently waiting.

That evening Polly Smith, drawing charts and diagrams, explains what she plans to do. Bill Smith is in full agreement. They only hope it will not be too late to save Gloria.

CHAPTER THIRTEEN

Before we come to our 'finale' with the 'murderous magistrates' we need to wrap up the last act in the drama of our English aristocrats. If we start with Boothby we can then move on to Elizabeth and Harold.

Bill Smith settles down to type.

We are in the summer of '64 and Bob Boothby has been elevated to the House of Lords with that splendid moniker Baron Boothby of Buchan and Rattray Head. He's also a panellist on radio and television programmes. He's witty, clever and popular. So he's riding high – certainly high enough to take a big old fall.

And this fall duly arrives when a Sunday newspaper reveals that it has the extremely juicy goods on a certain 'unnamed' peer. And everyone, over their Sunday breakfast table, looks at their spouse and says, 'Now I wonder who that can be, ha ha ha,' and they all have a giggle because it is great when one of the high-ups (they all know who it is) gets a dose of something smelly right in the face.

The newspaper says that this 'unnamed' and mysterious peer is consorting in an extremely sordid way with a couple of nasty London gangsters called the Kray Twins. So the newspaper is all cocky and crowy because it considers it has the 'unnamed' peer banged to rights. All the information comes from police sources and is 100 per cent guaranteed true, so the newspaper says. The article, actually, is more by way of a teaser or an aperitif, with full detail and pictures promised for the following weekend.

Does this article rock Boothby to the core as it should?

Not at all! Because what the poor old newspaper editor has not realised is that, while Boothby is affable and friendly and witty and so on and so on, like all aristocrats and others of that ilk, he is extremely dangerous when cornered. In other words, Boothby doesn't stay all sly and in the shadows. Instead, what he does is to give a great big blast on his trumpet and shout 'charge!' In other words, he writes a letter to *The Times*. It's a paragon of erudition. He reveals himself as the peer in question but all allegations are refuted down to last tittle and jot. Then old Bob gets down and dirty and goes to work to stir the pot. The main thing he says, which is a massive bluff, is that he will sue to clear his name.

And boy does that send the wind billowing up the skirts of the political establishment! Because if there is a trial for libel a heck of a lot of political dirty linen is going to be washed in public. So the lawyers and the fixers go in and play it hard and dirty, putting the frighteners on and getting the result they want.

But of course the readers of the Sunday newspaper do not know anything of this. They are waiting expectantly for the next Sunday so they can have another good giggle and watch the roof finally fall in on the dirty old rogue. And they are right in one way about that roof falling in.

So now imagine the editor of our newspaper. He is sitting at his desk, rubbing his hands. In front of him are the galley proofs of the scoop which is going to finish off the old rogue Boothby. He is probably even humming a little tune. But at that moment there is a call from the top floor. Up to see his boss is our editor summoned. And the interview is short, sharp and not at all sweet.

'Clear your desk, sir, and never darken my door again. You are a maker-up of false tales, a listener to police lies, tittle-tattle and gossip.'

The next scene is easy to picture. It is the poor old editor, scratching his head as he leaves the building, wondering at the tornado that has come out of a clear blue sky to bring down that roof on him.

And it is a puzzle as well to the readers of the Sunday newspaper. Because on the front page is a big old apology, enough to make your jaw drop. It might as well have read: 'WORLD TURNED ON HEAD'. And it might as well have continued, for all the sense it made, 'All got it wrong we. Sincere and bumble apologies. Editor who listened to tittle-tattle been sent to mine salt in USSR. Because as any one know black is white and two and two is five. Whatever was we thinking?'

And here is the rib-tickler: the newspaper even agrees to pay Boothby £40,000 damages for hurt feelings and damage to reputation, etc. In today's money that is about half a million quid!

And here is another aside which shows the strange world in which people like Boothby live. He ends up writing cheques to friends and good causes for in excess of the £40,000 and so gets himself into another financial mess! In other words, it's possible to be both genius and fool at the same time.

So how do we unravel this particular ball of string? As Elizabeth would say, who put the fix in?

Because when the detail does finally come out, a few years later, we see that actually the newspaper didn't have the half of it. What it shows is that Boothby is a risk-taker like you can't imagine. You could say it's a drug for him. Perhaps it is the same need for risk and adventure that motivates people like Jack London.

There is so much detail.

Boothby really does invite the violent East End gangster, Ronnie Kray, to dine with him in the House of Lords in full view of all the snobby lords and ladies. And after their dinner they really do set off, the pair of them, quite openly to trawl some extremely seedy nightclubs. And the Kray Twins (Ronnie and Reggie) really do provide what are then called 'male lovers' for Boothby. Remembering of course, Dear Reader, that 'male lovers' are very much illegal at the time. For that sort of thing you could easily, like Oscar Wilde, end up in jail. And the Eaton Square residence really is set up for spectacular (men-only) sex orgies with joint masters of ceremonies the Kray Twins and their new best friend Baron Boothby of Buchan and Rattray Head! The orgies are so popular it is 'stand back and form an orderly queue' to get in!

Bill Smith wonders if Gordon the Butler was in attendance and, if so, in what capacity? Did he just serve the champagne? And does (as Bill Smith imagines) Baron Boothby direct operations while sitting crossed-legged on a sofa, in the manner of an immense Buddha, with not a stitch on aside from an orange turban wrapped around his fat head?

Actually, levity aside, much of the detail would probably turn your stomach and is best left out. But here is the shorthand answer to the question you are no doubt asking about the whys and wherefores of the scandal. It's the dates that are important.

As stated earlier, we are in the summer of 1964. The establishment is still recovering from the Christine Keeler scandal of two years before, a heady mix of Russian spies, politics and saucy sex, which almost brings down Harold Macmillan's government. The current PM, still a Tory, is Alec

Douglas-Home. But the young Labour leader, Harold Wilson, is on the rise and looking for power. The problem for Wilson is that one of the MPs in his inner circle is also an attender at the Eaton Square orgies. His name is Tom Driberg and he is a louche character who drinks too much and who on occasion, so it is rumoured, passes titbits of information to his friends in the KGB. Ergo no one – neither Wilson nor Douglas-Home – wants the scandal a Boothby libel trial would bring. That's why the pressure is brought to bear on the proprietor of the Sunday newspaper – or, as Elizabeth would say, 'the fix is put in'.

Don't be too scandalised, Dear Reader. It's a story as old as the hills.

There is a simple compact: the ruling class provides us with our security and in turn we let them get away with things that would send lesser people to jail. We accept their greed and all the rest of the antics. Actually, we like having a toff such as Boothby ruling over us. We like a bit of class driving round in his Roller. Do you want someone like your sour-faced neighbour running the country?

So what happens to Boothby – the gambler, the risk-taker, the man who so publicly cuckolded his friend Harold Macmillan for well on thirty years? And the man, we should remember, who if he had he played his cards better might have been PM himself. Well up he comes, smelling if not quite of roses then something not far off, to retain his position as our slightly tarnished but still much-loved national treasure.

Bill Smith takes the last page out of the old Underwood typewriter and reads it carefully. That was the easy bit. Getting down the story of Elizabeth and that Grave Constitutional Crisis is going to be more difficult. Bill Smith has several stabs at it before finally writing: Harold and Dorothy are spending the week at Balmoral. Elizabeth always receives the prime minister of the day, and his wife, over the summer at her Scottish residence.

Then Bill Smith stops. He taps the side of the old Underwood typewriter with his pencil and frowns. The trick is to get the register right. Too 'over the top' and people will say, 'Oh another clever dick having a go at the monarchy,' and give a great big yawn and turn to something else.

Bill Smith opens a diary that Roger kept, which on occasion he has been using to crib certain detail. On the first page Roger has written and underscored, 'This diary confided to Haiku on my passing. Please keep private! Risk of Grave Constitutional Crisis if made public.' On the next page he is recounting a lunch he had with Elizabeth. Roger, so he says, is telling Elizabeth an amusing little story about the Japanese foreign minister who, apparently, is known among the secretaries as Mr Wandering Hands.

Bill Smith skips forward a couple of pages and stops.

The royal staff are in almost open revolt. A rude ditty about Boothby's sexual preferences has apparently been circulating among staff at Sandringham. Then the cleaning staff at Windsor, so it is said, discover a cartoon of Macmillan wearing a pair of cuckold's horns, which is pinned to a chair in a stateroom. Then to top it all, according to Roger's 'sources', women on the royal staff at Balmoral are threatening to hoist certain of Dorothy Macmillan's undergarments up a flag pole to show their disapproval of the 'activities' of that particular lady!

Bill Smith cracks a sly smile and moves on.

The diary is full of other racy scuttlebutt. Roger gives a very tart evaluation of Philip. He says it was well known on the Tokyo cocktail circuit that Philip regularly squired low grade 'actresses' round certain rather louche London clubs.

As to the courtiers who surround Elizabeth, Roger notes in the diary that they are, 'far worse than you can imagine'. 'Really low grade nitwits' is his undiplomatic phrase. The reason for these criticisms is of course that Roger, as everyone knows by now, is 'cute' on Elizabeth himself. There are frequent mentions in the diary of Elizabeth's 'luminosity' and her *joie de vivre*. So naturally he is defensive when he sees her badly served by others. But if we're to get a proper grip on Elizabeth's psyche we have to remember the close relationship she had with her father, King George, Bill Smith writes, at the same time keeping in mind that Harold is also of King George's generation.

So now we come to the final scene. The detail is largely taken from Roger's diary.

It is the second day of Harold and Dorothy's visit to Balmoral. Lunch is over. Dorothy has pleaded a headache and is in her room and the 'awful Mr Windsor' has also taken himself off elsewhere. It's a warm afternoon so Elizabeth and Harold have decided to take a walk together in the grounds.

They fall into an easy step. As people do, they are talking about their families. Harold is worried about his son, Maurice, who has the Cavendish disease of alcoholism. And of course there is the youngest daughter, poor Sarah, who has always been a problem. In fact, all the children have been affected by the Boothby business. In turn, Elizabeth is confiding her worries about the succession. It's no secret that she favours Anne over Charles.

The couple have finally halted in the wonderfully named Rose Bower. It is a discreet glade with a carved bench and overhanging bushes and trailing flowers. They sit down on the bench and Elizabeth takes up the conversation. Of course they should have been more discreet, Bill Smith types. Even in the private grounds of Balmoral there are always secret service agents watching.

The incident itself is described with perfect brevity as, 'Hand on knee followed by light embrace.'

Bill Smith stops and repeats the line aloud several times. It has a cadence, like a dance instruction. But Roger gives no clue in the diary as to who made the first move. Whose hand was it on whose knee?

Bill Smith gets up and goes into the kitchen to ask Polly but remembers she has gone to see Madame Solaris for a card reading.

He sits down again and picks up the diary. Could Macmillan have been tried for treason? Bill Smith imagines crowds in the street shouting for his head to be off-chopped. (Until kinder times arrive and he is exhumed and his head is found, wherever it was put. So finally he, and his head, are given a decent funeral and people line the streets full of sympathy because he was a man who was greatly wronged by his wife, Dorothy. There is sympathy, too, for Elizabeth who had to put up with the 'awful Mr Windsor' for so long.) Bill turns to the next page in the diary and comes to Roger's warning about a 'ticking time bomb'.

Roger is convinced that if the story comes out while she is still alive Elizabeth will have to abdicate. That makes Bill Smith stop short. He lives in France, so he might observe the British monarchy with a certain detached amusement, but he does not want to be the cause of its downfall. He looks at the diary and then touches it with his hand. 'I had better guard that,' he says to himself, quietly.

Bill Smith pauses and then decides to add a final scene.

It's Roger's funeral. Quiet country church. East Anglia. Rooks cawing, wind blowing through the trees. Haiku and his wife and their daughter are in the front pew and there are only a dozen or so other attendees. There is no royal presence. A distant cousin follows the vicar to say a few kind words and there are a couple of hymns. At the back of the church are two gents in suits. They move lightly on their feet for big men. Bulges in suit jackets indicate they are 'carrying'. Outside the church they approach Haiku. One of them whispers in his ear, 'You need to hand over the diary and keep your mouth zipped, buddy. If not it's the concrete suitcase for you.'

To which Haiku – he is his father's son – turns sharply on his heel and walks away.

Bill Smith stops and reads back what he has written. He hesitates and worries that he has not got the tone right. Then he looks at his watch. He needs to get ready.

It will soon be time for Bill and Polly Smith to set out on their night's adventure.

CHAPTER FOURTEEN

Well here we go, Dear Reader; Bill and Polly Smith are finally off to the races. Finally off to start their new career as criminals! And their hearts are going *jig jig jig* and their stomachs are going *jug jug jug*. In other words, they are nervous as hell.

For this criminal venture Polly Smith has selected anoraks in muted colours as dress for both of them. Balaclavas will be put on at the last moment. They have ropes and ingenious housebreaking gadgets tucked away inside lightweight backpacks. When all your family are circus performers, getting hold of these sorts of gadgets and implements is not a problem.

In relation to timing Polly Smith, who is very much in charge of the operation, has made a fine calculation. She has chosen an hour late enough so they can operate under cover of darkness, but still early enough so that the two magistrates will be out on the town, as it's a Friday evening, and will not return to disturb them.

Bill and Polly Smith do not take the tram or risk showing themselves in the brightly lit Quartier de la Gare. Instead, the intrepid criminals make their way on foot down the Cours de la Marne. Then they twist and turn through narrow side streets, keeping to shadows and avoiding well-lit areas, until they are in

Nansouty and can see the outline of the L'Église de Sacré Coeur.

Polly Smith has already ruled out attempting to enter through the front of the house as the street is lit and there are cars going up and down. However, she has noted from her previous reconnaissance that the front door is partially glazed, so they make a quick covert swing past the front and note with relief no light shining inside.

So now they are ready.

The criminal pair, led by Polly 'The Cat' Smith, are standing at the back of the magistrates' house in the shadow of the church. Did Bill Smith say before that the house is one of those old-fashioned single-storey row houses known in Bordeaux as échoppe houses? The pair of criminals stand on the steps of the church, which gives them that bit of elevation so they can see over the garden wall. Through a back window that is not shuttered they see once again, to their relief, no lights on inside.

But this is still not a piece of cake, Dear Reader; actually it is quite an operation that is being sized up by this criminal duo. But they know all the precautions they must take. For a start, you must always wear gloves and a hat and you also should not let any bare skin touch an interior surface. Everyone knows today that if you give a policeman a fibre of hair you are soon going to be before a judge and going to prison for a long time, so at the end of the operation you must destroy all the clothing you have worn. But these are things you already know, Dear Reader. You read the detective novels and watch the crime movies, same as everyone else. At the same time you must be prepared for the unexpected. There are always hitches to the best-laid plans.

So Polly Smith has removed a length of rope and a grappling hook from her backpack and is about to cross the street to the house when she suddenly freezes, because what has happened

— just like in the movies — is that the moon has come out from behind a cloud and suddenly the whole street is bathed in that silvery light. So the pair are thinking they may have to abandon the whole operation but then the moon retires back behind its clouds and they can continue.

How Jack London would have loved that interlude! Jack London loved to fly by the seat of his pants. But for poor old Bill Smith it is a case of his stomach going *jug jug jug* once more.

After that it is game on.

Polly 'The Cat' Smith counts to five and the pair of them pull their balaclavas down over their faces. Then they cross the street and Polly Smith throws the grappling iron up so that it hooks over the garden wall. She does a quick pull to test that it is holding and then hauls herself up. Her lithe physique and circus-trained nimbleness are an advantage here, Bill Smith types. Then she scrambles over the top of the wall and drops down into the small back garden. Bill Smith holds his breath but there is no startled cry, no sudden turning on of lights or bark of a dog or anything like that. Then the back gate is opening and Bill Smith is slipping through the opening like a phantom of the night …

In the garden they freeze for a further count of ten before approaching the house.

Then Polly 'The Cat' Smith takes from her backpack a small suction cup gadget, which she attaches carefully to the window pane. Then, using a cutter attached to the suction cup, she cuts a circular hole and pulls out the glass, all without making a sound. Then Polly puts a hand inside and undoes the latch on the window. Then she is up on the sill and dropping down inside the house, where she freezes for another count of ten. Still hearing nothing, she opens the door to let Bill Smith inside.

In any criminal operation a moment of adjustment is important. In this case the criminal pair wait until they have gained their night vision and factored in any background noises. It is then they discover that they are in the kitchen. They can see, in the dim light coming from the window, that the two magistrates are tidy enough in a rudimentary way – plates are stacked and so on. But Polly Smith notes that a female presence is missing. So this is certainly a bachelor pad.

Now they are in the passage leading out of the kitchen and they can see there are two doors to their right, both of which are slightly ajar. Everyone knows there is a terrible danger in opening a door in an old house. This is because there is a racing certainty that it is going to creak. But Polly 'The Cat' Smith is so delicate and sure-footed that she is able to open the doors to the bathroom and the bedroom – just wide enough to put her head around – without making a sound and thereby ascertain that both rooms are empty.

So now they go slowly down the passage towards the front door. This passage opens out into a space which is actually the living room. There are shutters pulled across the windows but light filters in from the street through the partially glazed front door.

At this stage they are conducting the operation entirely by hand signals. Neither one of this criminal pair has spoken a word since they entered the house. Polly Smith takes a low-powered hand torch from her backpack. She has masked half the beam with tape and scopes it low over the floor. This is the scene the torch lights up: two armchairs drawn up in front of a television; to the left a waste bin, half-full with crushed beer cans. To the side of the television is a DVD player with a small rack of DVDs on top of it. Scattered on the floor between the television and the armchairs are several paperback books.

The sight of the books sends a shiver down Bill Smith's spine; his worst fears are confirmed.

'Christ,' he says softly. 'They're bloody readers.'

He signals to Polly and she points the torch at the books. One of them is certainly the dog-eared paperback he had seen in the pocket of the Boy. Carefully he turns it over with his foot. Polly shines the torch on it: *The Outsider* by Albert Camus.

Bill Smith draws in his breath. The hunch he had been reluctant to formulate earlier is proving correct.

Bill Smith perches on the edge of one of the arm chairs. By the dim light of the torch he explains, 'Young French guy in colonial Algeria. Sometime after the war. Kills an Arab. Court condemns him to death because he doesn't show remorse, bow the head, etc. Appears not to give much of a damn about anything. Used as an excuse by misunderstood youth to demand liberty and promote non-conformity.'

Bill Smith turns over another book with his foot. *Crime and Punishment*. He gives another grimace and swears softly again.

'Same thing. Student in Russia kicks over the traces. Thinks he is exceptional. Tops old woman with an axe. Again rusk-fed youths use it as their text to show their exceptionalism, no need to obey laws, etc.'

As he talks, Jackson Pollock-style electrical charges are racing through the tendrils of Bill Smith's brain. They will soon be out in the open, sparking furiously. Polly Smith is telling him, in a low voice, that they need to complete their mission and get out of the house as quickly as possible. Bill Smith bends down to the DVD player and takes out a disc. He holds it up to the light of Polly Smith's masked torch with his gloved hand and reads out loud, '*Pickpocket*. A film by Robert Bresson.'

He pulls a face.

'Same bloody nonsense. Pickpocket going around thinking he's a cut above. God save us from the young when they are being deep and meaningful.' He riffles through the other DVDs on top of the player.

'Scorsese … Tarantino … All the usual suspects.' The brain tendrils are now sparking like exposed cables in a storm. He signals Polly Smith to sit down in the other arm chair. He says, 'I'll make it as quick as I can.' His voice is serious. 'We've mentioned it before. It's called the compact.'

Polly looks at him hard.

'Works every time. Has done through history. It works for any group, from family through to country. Groups always divide up into leaders and led. Call it the elite and the people.'

He is settling into his explanation.

'The people want security. Want to get on with their lives. Do business. Have families, bring up children, all that. So the elite – they can be church, aristocracy, Communist Party, big business, army, even patriarchal family head – they say, "Don't worry; we can take care of that." But of course the elite don't provide this security for nothing. They want a tribute. The tribute can take different forms. Sometimes it's a tax. More often it is just a larger share of the pie. So the people pay the tribute and the elite organise the security. That's the compact. That's the way the world works.'

He looks at Polly.

'Remember we talked about Jackson Pollock and those fractals? Those patterns that reappear endlessly in nature? Well the compact is like that. It's the pattern in the background. All shapes and sizes. Big and small. At the moment, for the purposes of government, we call it democracy.'

Bill Smith is aware that with every passing minute the danger of discovery increases. Polly Smith is looking anxiously at her watch. Bill Smith considers and then continues.

'People like to be ruled by their 'betters'. That's another important point to remember. They don't want to be ordered about by someone who looks like their brother-in-law. That is why they don't object when the elite gobble up a larger share of the pie. They also allow the elite to take liberties forbidden to others. It shows they have got class. In turn, the elite don't mind if the people let off steam once in a while. Football matches and so on.'

Polly is looking increasingly anxious.

Bill Smith presses on.

'The compact works well when it's all in balance but it's a delicate beast. If the elite doesn't provide proper security, or takes too many liberties, or demands too much tax, the people get restless. On the other hand, if the people make excessive demands the elite can also get anxious.'

Polly Smith nods her head. She is beginning to get the point.

'So Harold and Elizabeth are examples of leaders who have kept the compact. Acted fairly and not taken too much. Remembered their duties and obligations and so on. And Boothby and Dorothy Macmillan and Philip and the Cavendishes and John Bodkin Adams and certainly the Kray Twins are examples of people who have taken too much and abused the compact?'

Bill Smith smiles.

'Sure, that's the general idea. But a lot of people would say you are being too generous as to where you have placed the dividing line.'

He pauses before continuing, 'The compact has to have its enforcers, people who make sure the rules are kept. That's where the judges come in. Most of the time it's bread and butter stuff, humdrum. They go by the book. But if there is a crisis they have to come down hard.'

Bill Smith nods towards the books on the floor.

'The young guy in *The Outsider*. Doesn't show remorse for his crime. Doesn't mourn his mother's death. Says he doesn't believe in God. So he's not playing the game. He's an individualist who's indifferent to the rules. So that's why the jury convicts him and the judge sends him to the guillotine. We're supposed to sympathise with him. The kids of today see him as a hero. They're all individualists. They think they're the exceptional people exempted from conformity and tradition.

'But the judge wants the magistrates to draw the opposite conclusion to the regular reader. He wants them to believe that the judge and the jury got it right. Because by refusing to conform, the man is threatening the compact. And if everybody kicks over the traces and refuses to respect tradition where will the compact be? There'll be chaos. We'll all be in the gutter looking up at the stars.

'So the judge is telling the young magistrates that they are the guardians of the compact. The enforcers, if you like. In other words, in time of crisis, they may be called on to act very roughly.'

Bill Smith takes a deep breath.

'So the judge tells the young magistrates to commit a random murder. He is toughening them up to join the elite. He's showing them that, *in extremis*, anything – even murder – is permissible to defend the compact. When he's finished with them, like the judge in *The Outsider*, they won't be afraid to make an example.'

Polly Smith then says slowly, 'Well, hold on. That's not much different from a young Mafiosi committing a murder to make his bones.'

That makes Bill Smith laugh out loud.

'Actually that Mafia analogy certainly has a lot going for it,' he says.

(And, by the way, there is currently the debate about whether there will be a 'levelling up' after the Great Plague. Not a bit of it, says Bill Smith. There will always be an elite offering security in return for a tribute. It is just the way the world works.)

Then Polly Smith says, 'Well hold on, what about the other stories and the characters like the Norwegian Flyer and the English Rose and Madame Solaris and Goya and Jackson Pollock and Otto Dix and Carl Jung and Jack London and Michel de Montaigne and the back page of *Sud Ouest*?'

Bill Smith laughs again.

'Oh, that was to show that, most important of all, the world is a great and wonderful place full of mad and unexpected surprises.'

After that things begin to move swiftly, Bill Smith types.

All readers know that the best friend of novelists is the flawed criminal mind. Every criminal who comes to a sticky end can look back on his (or her) criminal act and see where the critical mistake was made. In Bill and Polly Smith's case their undoing was, of course, not to check the small broom cupboard on the left-hand side as they walked down the passageway. They had been so intent on checking the bedroom and bathroom they had missed it entirely.

Anyhow, what happens is that as Bill Smith is coming to the end of his discourse on the compact they both hear, at the same time, a squeak and a movement coming from the passageway. Bill Smith looks up and Polly Smith shines the torch across the passageway and sees the door of the broom cupboard.

Then Polly Smith is up on her feet, followed by Bill Smith, and she has taken a step across the room and is opening the cupboard door in the passageway opposite the bedroom and flicking the torch forward. And of course, Dear Reader, you have guessed it because perched on a stool in the cupboard, among the mops and pails and with a rough gag in her mouth and bound hand and foot, is dear Gloria from Patisserie Solaris.

So they rush forward and by the light of the torch they unbind her and remove the gag and she collapses into their arms, tears of exhaustion and relief streaming down her face.

Understandably, Gloria is unaware of the delicacy of the situation and the need for caution and silence. And when you have been trussed up like a turkey and left in a broom cupboard for heaven knows how long and when a couple of kind souls find you and release you the first thing you're going to do when the gag is removed is give a whoop, which certainly counts as a real loud noise in a silent house.

As this whooping is happening Bill Smith feels his stomach going *jug, jug, jug* once again. He knows they have to get out of the house with Gloria right now.

But for the moment Gloria is not to be stopped. She is hanging around their necks and telling them, through sobs, that the two magistrates had been planning – she had overheard them talking – to throw her off the Pont de Pierre. But something had happened, they had to go home for the weekend, so they had tied her up here and told her not to make a noise and that they would come back on Monday and deal with her then.

With all this racket going on Bill Smith fails to hear, although Polly Smith clocks it straightaway, that noise which, in the crime movies, is always accompanied by a change in the music. And everyone's heart misses a beat and they are all on the edge of their seats. Because the noise that Polly Smith hears is of course the turning of a key in the front door ...

And then the front door opens and the main light is switched on and in the glare of the light they are all standing there frozen to the spot. It would have made a good still life tableau. It would certainly have been entitled *Caught In The Act*.

Then Polly Smith shouts, 'Run for it,' and Bill Smith, for once in his life acting swiftly, picks up the broom and a mop and a pail that are in the cupboard and hurls them in the direction of the two magistrates, who are still standing in the doorway, trying to work out what in the hell is going on here.

And of course on the step behind them is the old judge himself and he is looking pretty bloody poleaxed as well.

So suddenly, after this split second of inactivity, everything starts again with a rush.

The magistrates put their hands to their faces as the broom and the mop and the pail fly towards them, at the same time as Polly Smith and Gloria are running out of the back door, which they had left on the latch. Polly Smith, who is fleet of foot, is urging on poor Gloria, who is still tottering. They are followed by Bill Smith. They have a head start on the magistrates but over any distance they are bound to be caught.

So here is what happens next, Dear Reader.

The three of them are running down the street as fast as they can with the two magistrates and the old judge in hot pursuit. The magistrates and the judge are in a sweat because they know if Bill and Polly Smith and Gloria escape and tell their story they will have to do some fancy talking to avoid being in the dock themselves.

So when they reach a turning in the road Bill Smith hisses to Polly Smith, 'Go left! I will go right and act as a decoy.' So Polly Smith, realising and appreciating the heroic sacrifice her husband Bill Smith is making (she will recount the story later with a considerable degree of pride and a real warm feeling in her heart), scoots down a side alley with Gloria. Bill Smith pauses for a moment to make sure the pursuers have seen him and then sets off again. He is drawing their fire, as they say in military circles.

When he glances over his shoulder he sees that his ruse has worked and that the two magistrates and the judge are in pursuit of him. At the same time he can feel his old ticker bursting, along with his lungs. In desperation, he ducks down a series of back streets in the direction of the river but those legal gentlemen are still doggedly on his tail.

Then he looks over his shoulder and sees that they are gaining on him and one of them has something in his right hand. That something is certainly a gun and it is pointing at Bill Smith.

Summoning a last burst of energy (he thinks of the poor Inuit lady who died in the plane crash and who had saved her children displaying what is called hysterical strength) he takes a last turn down to the river – to find himself in a blind alley.

As he stops, panting, cornered, his heart bursting, his thoughts are only for Polly Smith and his love for her. He realises that for once in his life he has acted heroically.

At the same time he hears the sound of the pounding feet coming up from behind and getting ever louder. Next thing, his arms are being grabbed and he is being forced up against the wall.

'Where's the girl?' the Fox demands. But Bill Smith, girding his loins, refuses to answer.

Then he hears the Boy shout, 'You interfering bastard, you will pay for this!'

The two magistrates have Bill Smith in a vice-like grip up against the wall. He can hear more footsteps approaching and he knows the judge is behind him.

The last thing he feels is the barrel of the pistol being jabbed into the back of his neck. The last thing he hears is the sound of the pistol being cocked.

Then a shot rang out ... and a body fell into the water.

THE END

Also by Rorie Smith

Tombola! — ISBN: 978-0-992950-33-0

When 15,000 children are starving to death every day is it legitimate to do nothing? When a businessman becomes a tyrant with no redeeming features is it justifiable to kill him? No? Not even if he threatens to demolish your football club to build a new print works for his newspaper? These are questions that Arthur Polianski, photocopier salesman, must face after receiving 'bad news' from his doctor. Spurred into action, Arthur investigates Billy Petersen's background and finds that the destruction of Athletic Football Club is only a minor misdemeanour in the catalogue of his crimes. But how to stop him? The solution seems obvious.

Extreme, angry, funny, absurd, and ultimately very human, Arthur is a great comic hero, the embodiment of all of us who have been put upon and who have dreamed of fighting back.

'A rattling good read' – Tribune

'Destined to be that rare type of book that people will talk about years from now' – BookLore

Counterpart — ISBN: 978-0-992950-30-9

A decorated World War Two hero and a beautiful Thai lady who has suffered for twenty-five years with Parkinson's disease are both dead. They are my father and my wife. This is a memoir of their lives. It is a love story, a story of adventure, a comedy and an homage. There is gambling, a gun, a bizarre manuscript. It is an attempt, by means of fiction, to be true to the spirit of who they were. It is also an attempt to preserve their memory for generations future. Because if we forget those who have gone before us we forget our history. And if we do not know our history how can we know ourselves? *Counterpart* is also an acknowledgement that there are as many different ways to see a life, or to write a memoir, as there are stars in the sky.

One Million Euro — ISBN: 978-0992950323

A group of pilgrims, led by the long-dead poet Walt Whitman and the legendary football manager Sir Roy Babadouche, are walking the Camino de Santiago. In the group are Echo the African Autodidact, Jack the Devon publican and an unlikely bank robber called Oscar Bebbington. Also in the group are a socialist climber called Wilson, a dentist by the name of Denis Dennis and Venezia, a jolie Quebecoise. Two donkeys carry their equipment. They are very modern pilgrims as none of them believe in God. Instead they declare: 'We are on pilgrimage to regain our humanity.' The group start their pilgrimage near Marciac in southern France, crossing into Spain via the Col du Somport. Their journey, a distance of 650 miles, takes them a total of 54 days. *One Million Euro* recounts their many and strange adventures. During the course of the journey the pilgrims also tell stories of their lives. Some of these stories are true, but others are made up.